MY DECEMBER DARLING

A SMALL-TOWN CHRISTMAS NOVELLA

NEW YORK TIMES BESTSELLING AUTHOR

LAUREN ASHER

To those who were torn between Doctors
McSteamy and McDreamy…
Get ready to fall in love with Doctor Darling.

Receta de Coquito
Familia Martinez

shake it before
... taste it

Con mi burrito sabanero,
voy camino de Belen

I'm just gonna keep on
waiting underneath the
mistletoe

Playlists

Scan the code

⏪ ◻️ ▷ ⏩

My December Darling

catch flights, not feelings

Welcome to the Night Shift

Coquito & Chill

The Happily Ever After playlist

Don't care about the
presents underneath the
Christmas tree

Blanco es mi quimera
Y es mensajera de paz y de
pure amor

El lucerito mañanero
ilumina mi sendero

Wisteria

shake it before you taste it

CHAPTER ONE

Catalina

"Look! There's Aiden now!" My sister, Gabriela, waves her hand in the direction of the hostess stand.

It's impressive how quickly she ruins my mood in less than five words, and no amount of Christmas music blasting from the speakers throughout the restaurant will save me.

"He's joining us?" I grip the back of my chair tightly instead of taking my seat at the table like we were about to.

Gabriela's brows scrunch together. "Yeah. I texted you about it yesterday."

Shoot. I turned on the Do Not Disturb setting because Mom kept hounding me with questions about my maid of honor speech. While I haven't managed to write a sentence yet, Aiden's best man, Luke Darling, already sent my mom a copy for her to approve.

"Is Aiden joining us going to be a problem?" My sister asks in a somewhat

strained tone. Mom's gaze bounces between the two of us, accusatory as ever when it lands on me, silently demanding that I don't cause a scene and ruin my sister's day.

"No," I fight to transform my frown into a smile. "No issue at all."

It's a lie, but thankfully, no one calls me out on it. To say things have been slightly awkward between my sister and me since she started dating my ex is an understatement, but then again, I haven't helped matters either.

Which is why you're here, making an effort to be present and helpful before Gabriela's wedding instead of avoiding everyone until right before the rehearsal dinner.

My expression must ease my sister's concerns because she quickly turns toward the restaurant's front door.

Her smile returns. "Oh good! Luke decided to come after all."

I was so distracted by my thoughts that I didn't notice Luke strolling into the restaurant behind Aiden.

Shit.

My heart falters. "He's here too?"

Gabriela glances over at me. "He and Aiden had plans, so I invited him."

"Why?" The question accidentally slips out.

I may have only spoken to Luke on four separate occasions, but it was enough. I've dated guys like him in the past, and it never ended well for me, so I prefer to stay away from Luke and his chronic cheerfulness.

Well, I should steer clear because of that and the fact that he is Aiden's attractive, intelligent, sweet best friend from medical school. I never met him until *after* Aiden broke up with me because Doctor Darling was busy volunteering with the Red Cross.

The man really is perfect on paper, and the exact kind of person my mother would want me to date...*if* I was even open to dating someone from Lake Wisteria.

Technically, Luke isn't from our small town, but he moved here a year ago because of Aiden and a job opening at the hospital, so I'm lumping him in with all the other men here.

"Cata," Mom says my nickname like a curse.

"Yes?" I snap while glaring at her.

She turns her nose up in clear displeasure. "Can you manage to not cause a scene for an hour?"

I ignore the slice of pain in my chest and plaster a bored expression on my face. "I don't know. It's a difficult request..."

Gabriela releases an exasperated sigh.

Mom huffs. "I don't understand your reasons for disliking Luke, but he's practically Aiden's family, so would it kill you to be nice?"

The jab lands, although I'm careful not to show it. I'm not even sure Mom is aware of how much those kinds of statements hurt me because I've never opened up to her about it.

"Princess," Aiden announces as soon as he reaches our table. His blond hair has been recently cut, and he is dressed in his usual polo and pressed khakis, looking like he strolled out of a country club. Aiden's choice of attire should have been the first sign of us not being a good match, but I thought his style was exactly what my mother would like.

It didn't take me long to realize I was dating Aiden for

all the wrong reasons, especially in the hope of appeasing my mother, and he seemed to feel similarly about us, although he had the courage to break things off with me first.

My future brother-in-law wraps his arms around Gaby and pulls her against his chest. She sinks into him when he drops a kiss on the top of her head, earning a little sound of appreciation from my mother, and the smallest smile from me.

I'll be the first to admit they're pretty damn cute together, even if Aiden's little pet name for Gaby makes my eyes roll from time to time.

I'm so distracted by the two lovebirds that I miss Luke walking around the table until his arm brushes against mine. A light, airy sensation builds inside of my chest from a single touch, right before I crush it with the weight of our reality.

I might *like* Luke's touch. I might even *like* the way he smells like sandalwood and leather from the jacket he is currently wearing over a plain black Henley and jeans. But I *dislike* Luke the person. He's annoyingly friendly, frustratingly thoughtful, and the kind of guy who could inspire a future comic book superhero, thanks to both his muscles and his commitment to helping others.

"Catalina," Luke says my name with a smile. I'm not surprised, seeing as he gives everybody the same one.

Something about the way his smile makes me *feel* sets off alarms in my head, and I add some space between us.

"Lucas."

His grin expands as he turns to face me. "It's *Luke*."

"Huh. And here I thought we were calling each other by our full names."

He chuckles to himself, making my stomach flutter. "My name isn't Lucas."

"Shame. I like it better than *Luke*."

His brown eyes sparkle like they always do whenever he is amused, and damn, they really are pretty and framed by the darkest, thickest lashes that put mine to shame.

I have to break eye contact first, solely because I can't handle his attention.

Luke Darling might live up to his last name with everyone, but I'm not entirely convinced. I mean, there has to be something wrong with him, right? No one can be *that* happy all the time, or that willing to go out of his way to assist others, even if he is held to an oath to protect every life at all costs.

Regardless of my concerns, I'll have to put up with Luke for the foreseeable future since the two people we love are getting married, whether I like him or not.

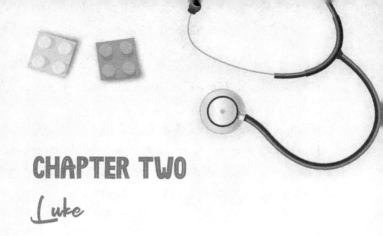

CHAPTER TWO

Luke

Despite the pep talk I gave myself during the walk over to the restaurant about being on my best behavior and acting like a mature man in my early thirties, the moment I saw Catalina, all bets were off.

We have only seen each other a handful of times since Aiden and Gaby have gotten together, and every single interaction has ended with me wondering why I bothered trying to talk to her in the first place. If Aiden hadn't insisted that I join them, I would've passed on lunch altogether.

Despite being roommates, it's rare for us to spend quality time together since we are both emergency room doctors at the new, state-of-the-art Lake Aurora hospital. Usually, we only see each other in passing since we both work graveyard shifts on different days, but today we both had the whole day off.

I thought I could get through today without incident, but clearly, I slipped up when I called Catalina

by her full name. She probably thought I did it strictly because I like to annoy her, but I just think her name is beautiful.

The waitress interrupts the table's conversation by asking for our orders. Everyone but me, the guy who didn't look at the menu because he was too focused on the beautiful, irritated brunette sitting across from him, knows what they want to eat, so I pick the first thing I see.

Catalina *snorts*, and hell, it sounds a lot cuter than it should.

Cuter? More like rude.

Yes. So damn rude, I find myself fighting both a smile and a request for her to repeat the sound again. Most people in town call Catalina an ice queen, but everyone has a melting point.

I just haven't found hers yet.

"Have something to share?" I lean forward on my elbows, giving her my full attention.

"Nope," she says with a pop of her lips. Her pink, pillowy, *always pulled into a frown whenever I'm around* lips.

"You sure about that?"

"Yup."

"Are all your conversations this riveting?"

"Possibly."

"Three whole syllables?" I check my pulse. "Warn a guy next time."

She stares down at her menu, pretending to read it despite already ordering her food. Aiden pulls me into a discussion he is having with Gabriela and her mom, all while Catalina watches with quiet interest. She doesn't say much whenever we are in a group setting, which only makes me more curious about whatever she is thinking.

Most likely silently judging you. I wouldn't put it past her, even if Aiden claims she is nice once you get to know her.

When our plates arrive, it doesn't take me long to understand why Catalina reacted the way she did when I placed my order. Had I known a Dragon's Breath roll would literally set my mouth on fire, I would have chosen something a bit more palatable. Literally, *anything* has to be better than the food currently burning through every last one of my taste buds.

At this rate, I might be the one needing to visit an emergency room because there is no way my stomach will make it through eating the entire plate of this.

I'd say it is the worst sushi roll on the planet, but with the way Catalina keeps laughing under her breath at me constantly chugging water between spells of heavy breathing, I would be lying.

I'm so caught up in the way her eyes sparkle that I'm taken aback when she reaches across the table and snatches a piece of sushi off my plate.

Before I can warn her against it, she tosses it into her mouth with a smile and chews.

No flinching. No watery eyes. No desperate search for water.

"Show off." I frown.

She gasps dramatically. "Did you just scowl?"

I glare.

"Whoa. Warn a girl next time." She mocks me by checking her pulse.

I flip her off with my chopstick, earning a little huff of

amusement from her and a choked laugh from Aiden sitting beside me. Gaby and Mrs. Martinez carry on the conversation, and I try to rejoin, only for Catalina to steal my attention again when she reaches over to eat another piece.

"You're such a baby. This is nothing," she says.

"If by nothing, you mean awful, then yes, we can finally agree on something for once."

She leans forward to take a third piece, but I pull my plate closer to me.

"Stop stealing my food."

Her eyes roll. "Is it considered stealing if you took one of mine when I wasn't looking?"

Shit. She noticed that?

I hold my hands up. "In my defense, I'm starving."

Her sigh is soft and resigned. "Here. We can trade." She doesn't wait for me to agree before swapping our plates. The move catches the attention of everyone at the table, although no one says anything.

Well, nobody except for *me*.

"Why did you do that?" I blurt out.

Her brows scrunch. "What do you mean *why*? You hate it."

"Yeah, well, you're not exactly known to be the nice sister, so I'm instantly suspicious." My tone is light and teasing, but with the way Catalina slinks back into her seat and avoids eye contact, I feel like a complete and utter jackass.

For once, we were having a pleasant conversation, and I ruined it without meaning to.

Her half-hearted shrug drills a hole through my heart. "You're right."

Then why have I never felt more wrong?

I'm irritated with myself as I say, "It was meant to be a joke."

"It's fine," she says with a clipped tone that confirms the complete opposite.

"Then why won't you look at me?"

It takes her a few seconds, but she manages to glance up from her plate. Her gaze flickers over my face. It lacks the warmth from a minute ago, leaving me yearning for…I'm not entirely sure, to be honest.

"Do you really want me to answer that question?" she asks.

"I wouldn't ask if I didn't." A playful smile tugs at my mouth.

Her gaze follows the gesture, and her brows crinkle together from how hard she frowns. "I find you…"

"Yes?" I lean in toward her, my breath catching in my throat as I wait for what she might say.

"Repugnant," she says with a small scrunch of her nose, as if the very idea of breathing the same air as me leaves a bad taste in her mouth.

"Repugnant?" Skepticism bleeds into every syllable. Never in my life has someone described me in such an insulting way, and definitely not after spending twenty minutes checking me out when they thought I wasn't paying attention.

Screw that. I've seen the way she stares at me, and *repugnant* is the last thing on her mind. That much I can promise.

She continues, "Yes. You're like a Captain America wannabe, and I don't mean that as a compliment."

My mouth falls open. "Excuse me?"

She releases a dramatic sigh. "I know it's hard to hear, given your savior complex."

Aiden, who apparently has been eavesdropping instead of listening to his future mother-in-law's story about visiting the dentist, chuckles under his breath.

"Shut up." I jab him in the ribs, making him wince.

He rubs at the spot. "You underestimate your superhero strength, *Captain America*."

The little she-devil across from me sits back in her seat with a satisfied smirk, and my heart trips at the sight. I'm not sure what kind of hold she has over me, but her presence is screwing with my head.

Up until this point, we've hardly spent time together. It was easy to coordinate having other plans since Catalina only visits Lake Wisteria twice a year, so I never thought to ask myself what would happen if I enjoyed her company.

And worse, how would I feel if I wanted more of it?

CHAPTER THREE

Catalina

O ur entire small town is in full-blown Christmas mode by the time my mom, sister, and I head toward the Thimble & Thread alterations shop after saying goodbye to Aiden and Luke. Within the hour it took for us to eat lunch, Main Street descended into complete mayhem, with a hundred volunteers helping set up the holiday decor for this weekend's Lake Wist-mas Holiday Extravaganza.

Cheery music softly plays from the speakers discreetly hidden along the road as a team of parents prepares hot chocolate to help volunteers fight against the brisk Michigan chill. Children run back and forth along the street, delivering paper cups to volunteers in the hope of securing their place on Santa's nice list.

Usually, Lake Wisteria lets its coastal-inspired buildings attract visitors, but during this time of year, the architecture is concealed by the thousands of Christmas lights, tinsel, massive lawn ornaments, and blow-up decor scattered around the busiest part of town.

I'm hit with childish excitement at the sight of so much holiday cheer, only for my happiness to be snuffed out at the number of people looking in our direction. Unlike my mom and sister, I'm not a people-person, so I prefer to hang back while they engage in painful small talk.

I stew in silence while they stop to talk to multiple people along the way to the alterations shop. Most are checking in to see when Mom will start selling *coquito* again, and she gives them all the details before playfully asking them not to report her and my dad to the sheriff for selling alcohol without a permit.

The Puerto Rican coconut drink has quickly become highly sought after in Lake Wisteria during the Christmas holiday season, outselling local eggnog vendors three years in a row.

I'm surprised Mom kept my dad's mom's holiday tradition alive since making *coquito* is a Martinez family thing, rather than from her side, but it makes me equal parts happy and sad to know my grandma's memory lives on in our small town.

By the time we make it to my sister's wedding dress fitting at Thimble & Thread alterations shop, I'm ready to call it a day, only to be dragged into small talk with my mom while sipping free champagne.

I watch Gaby with a mix of horror and fascination as she cries at her own reflection where she is trying on her dress for the second-to-last time before her big day on December 30th.

"It's so beautiful." A tear tracks down her cheek, clearing a watery path through her layer of foundation.

I exhale a sigh of relief. For a moment, I thought Gabriela was second-guessing her bedazzled tulle monstrosity of a dress that our dad paid for, but I should've known my sister would love to look like a princess straight out of a Dreamland movie. She even had her light brown hair styled today into the same updo she will be wearing on her wedding day in a few weeks' time, all so she could get a good idea of how she will look.

Mom, a former pageant queen whose dark hair has been permanently coifed for the last thirty years, rushes to dab at Gaby's cheek with a tissue. "You're ruining your makeup, *mi amor.*"

Despite Gaby being twenty-six years old, Mom treats her like a porcelain doll rather than a person with opinions, imperfections, and God forbid, *emotions*. It used to bother me, but I've grown to pity Gaby rather than envy her. It might have taken me a year's worth of therapy, but I've since learned that I'd much rather receive Mom's disapproval than her full, undivided attention.

In some ways, I even feel bad for my mom, knowing she holds herself to this high standard that sucks the joy out of life. I don't remember her always being this bad but growing up means gaining perspective on our parents and the fact that they're people too. People who can drive us crazy, but also people who can make mistakes and have flaws just like the rest of us.

And damn, does my mom have a flaw or two.

Gabriela does her best to fight the tears pooling at the bottom of her eyes but fails when she looks in the mirror again. I have to physically stop myself from laughing at her reaction by biting down on the inside of my cheek hard enough to make my own eyes water.

I love Gabriela, but that doesn't mean I won't hold back from an opportunity to tease her. It's practically expected of me, not only as her older sister, but as someone who took on the difficult task of helping her realize it's okay to make mistakes, take some risks, and live a life that makes her happy.

Looking back on it, maybe I taught Gabriela a little too well, seeing as she fell in love with the man I once dated. Thankfully, Aiden broke up with me before we slept together, or else I doubt Gaby would have bothered giving him the time of day.

Calling what Aiden and I had "a relationship" feels like a stretch when we had only been on a handful of dates. He was someone I had met while working at another hospital who happened to move to Lake Wisteria for a job earlier that year, and I was in town helping my family out while my dad recovered from a serious surgery. I wasn't sure if it would turn into anything, and deep down, a small part of me had hoped it might.

My selfish need to fill a void in my chest that yearns for a life partner led to hurting the one person I love most in this world, and I still hate myself for not noticing Gaby's crush on Aiden sooner. She clearly cared for Aiden long before I ever started casually dating him, but she never had the heart or self-confidence to tell me, let alone him. She was afraid he would reject her since they were good friends, so she stood by while he made a move on me.

It took Aiden breaking up with me to realize the negative

impact our relationship had on Gabriela, and I haven't stopped beating myself up over it ever since.

"Let's see how this looks with the dress." Mom's heeled booties click and clack against the floor as she walks over to my sister and places the faux fur bridal wrap around Gabriela's shoulders. Gaby wasn't sure about how it would look all together, but I can't think of a more perfect outfit for a winter wonderland wedding.

At first, I was skeptical about her having a wedding during the busiest time of the year, but Gaby wanted to get married on her and Aiden's anniversary date. Our family in Puerto Rico decided to make a whole trip out of it and come visit us for the holiday, so I guess it all worked out.

"What do you think?" Gaby turns and faces me.

Putting our different fashion tastes aside, she looks stunning, even if her makeup is a little heavier than usual, but that's not the reason why a painful knot forms inside my chest.

As the older sibling, part of me thought *I* would be the one to get married first, but Gaby beat me to it. I'm happy she found love, but the lack of it in my life makes me feel…sad? Lonely? Slightly hopeless, knowing I'm the reason I haven't found someone in the first place.

To put it bluntly, Aiden isn't the first man to find a reason to leave, but he was the one I couldn't escape by moving to a new city and taking on a temporary nursing job.

"Cata?" My sister asks with a furrowed brow.

"You look like a beautiful princess." I fight to get the words out without giving my emotions away.

"Really?" Gabriela's fake lashes tease her brow line with

how fast she is blinking.

"If a single compliment brings you to tears, I wonder what my maid of honor speech will do," I tease, hoping to ease some of my earlier heaviness.

"You have to write it first." Gabriela lets out a wet laugh.

"*Shh.*" I walk up to her and spin her around like we used to do when we were kids so we can both look at her reflection in the mirror. "Aiden is going to be beside himself when he sees you in this dress."

"You think so?"

"I *know* so. Plus, I already have a bet with the other bridesmaids about him crying during your first look, so I need him to pull through for me and have a full breakdown. Bonus if he pulls out a handkerchief."

Gabriela makes a face as she turns toward me. "You did not."

"Of course. Like I'd ever miss out on an opportunity to make a little money." I waggle my brows.

She frowns. "If I knew you were strapped for cash, I would've been happy to lend you some."

I give her a little shove, and we both laugh.

My mom gasps behind us. "Wait! We forgot the tiara!" She takes off running to the front door of the alteration shop, leaving Gabriela and me alone for the first time all day.

"God forbid we don't try on the tiara," I say, making Gabriela chuckle under her breath. "Seriously, how did you manage to not kill her while planning the wedding?"

"For the most part, it wasn't *too* bad."

"Except for the fact that you're having a church wedding

despite Aiden being an atheist."

Gabriela's *shush* comes out like a hiss. "Mami doesn't know that."

"She hasn't put two and two together yet with all those Masses you attend?"

"Nope. Aiden just dips his head and pretends he's praying the whole time. Works like a charm every Sunday."

"Let me guess. He's sleeping?" As someone who has a similar nocturnal schedule, I get it.

"Of course! Between paying for the wedding, saving up for a new house, and wanting to earn enough days to have a proper honeymoon, he's working every night shift possible."

I tuck a loose strand of her hair behind her ear. "He's a good guy."

"You would know since you dated him too."

Gabriela is the only one who can manage to make me laugh hard enough to make my eyes water.

She pulls me in for a hug. "I'm so happy you're sticking around for the whole month."

"Really?" I ask, somewhat surprised by my sister's confession. Ever since she got engaged, things have felt tense between us, so I expected her to be a bit more hesitant about my presence.

"Of course." My sister's cheeks flush. "And who knows. Maybe you love being back so much that you decide to stay longer."

"The agency is already reaching out to me about my plans for next year." I chose to be a traveling pediatric nurse for a reason, and it has nothing to do with how competitive the field is. Plus, I get to visit a bunch of new places, so what's not to love?

The loneliness, for starters.

I shove the thought aside.

"Do you have to leave so soon after I get married?" Her watery smile makes my chest tighten uncomfortably, so I respond in the only way I know how.

"You know me. Can't stay in one place for too long before I get the itch." Exploring new places through my camera lens has become my favorite pastime, and it's helped me step out of my comfort zone. I've met new people, learned to put myself out there, and shed some of my shyness in the process.

I can't imagine settling down in Lake Wisteria again. At least not *yet*.

I thought I'd have my life figured out before I came back. I'd hoped to meet someone special first, and I have serious doubts that it's going to be possible in our small town. Not to mention that I've sworn off all men from Lake Wisteria after everything that happened with Aiden and my sister.

It seems less messy and risky to search elsewhere.

And how is that going for you?

I press my lips together to stop myself from scowling. Constantly being on the move for my job means that I'm not able to build long-lasting connections, so I'm the only one to blame for my pitiful relationship status.

"It's so nice to have you home again though." My sister yanks me back into the conversation.

"Same." Visiting twice a year somehow feels like long enough in the moment, yet also never long enough as soon as

I leave.

"You know what? I'm going to make sure you have such a good time here that you'll never want to leave again."

"Best of luck," I say with a tight throat. I wouldn't put it past Gabriela to try, but there is no way I'm sticking around after she gets married.

No matter how much she wants me to.

CHAPTER FOUR

Luke

I finish wrapping up with a patient's chart when my phone vibrates in my pocket. Before I answer, I head to the nurses' station that was recently decorated with red-and-white striped wrapping paper. In the process of returning a pen I borrowed, I trip over a mini pine tree someone bought at the local grocery store but thankfully, none of the ornaments break.

"Hey, man," Aiden says as soon as I pick up the call.

"What's up?" I turn away from the counter.

"I need a favor."

Someone who sounds a lot like Gabriela is panicking in the background, spouting off about family members causing trouble and a cake.

"Everything okay?"

"Not really, but I'm hoping it will be. Can you cover my shift tomorrow? Please."

Fuck. The last thing I want to do

after an all-nighter tonight is repeat it tomorrow, but Aiden would do the same for me, no questions asked, so I nod, even though he can't see me. "Sure."

"Thanks. I'll return the favor whenever you want."

"Don't worry about it. Do you need any help? Besides the obvious, I mean."

He sighs. "No, but I appreciate it. Gabriela and I just need to sort out a little issue."

"Little?" Gabriela's voice gets louder. "The bakery lost our cake order!"

I wince. "Sounds like you've got it all covered."

"Wish me luck?"

"Forget luck. You need patience and a six-pack of beer ASAP."

Two back-to-back night shifts is killing me. My exhaustion worsens from one hour to the next, so I take a much-needed break and head to the coffee vending machine. There are a few strategically placed throughout the hospital, but my favorite one happens to be located on the fourth floor near the NICU.

It's quiet up here and far removed from the emergency room, so I can take a breather without worrying about a nurse coming to find me or someone yelling out codes in the background.

"Only a few more hours," I remind myself as I check for any updates from the nurses before taking a quick glance at my unopened messages on my phone.

The text thread I share with my parents is hardly used

throughout the year, unlike the one I was added to when Aiden's family unofficially adopted me a few years back. That chat is full of love, jokes poking fun at each other, and too many videos sent by Aiden's mother, covering a range of medical topics from the importance of gut health to cutting sugar from our diets.

MOM

Your father and I wanted to let you know that we won't be home for Christmas this year.

Of course not. My parents are rarely at the house I grew up in. Whether they are pulling long hours at their competing law firms or traveling for a conference, they have spent the majority of my life outside of the house, so I'm used to their absence.

More often than not, I wish my parents were more like Aiden's. They didn't have a lot of money, but they made up for it with enough love to make their kids *want* to return home for the holidays.

ME

Where are you going?

I send the text without expecting a reply, not since it's three in the morning, but because my parents hardly talk to me at all. Regardless of what they have planned, it's clear that I'm not invited to be part of it.

Dragging my feet, I walk over to the floor-to-ceiling window overlooking Lake Aurora and sip my sad, watery excuse for black coffee. This town is similar to Lake Wisteria, where I currently rent a small apartment with Aiden, although the town square lacks the same distinct coastal charm since it was remodeled back in the nineties. While the houses were preserved, the main business area was renovated, replacing history with glass structures that lack warmth or character.

Thankfully, their expansion project included the very hospital where Aiden and I work, so while I can't complain, I don't mind criticizing them for wiping out over a century of history.

A frustrated huff has me turning around to find a woman dressed in Christmas-themed scrubs jabbing her finger against the latté button three times. Gingerbread men are scattered across the cotton scrub top while the bottoms are a plain forest green. I swear I don't mean to ogle, but her perfect ass shakes from side to side as she leans forward to read the tiny letters on the machine.

My nails dig into the Styrofoam cup as I chastise myself for checking out another employee like this.

Yet you can't seem to take your eyes off her.

She stabs at the same broken latté button and curses in Spanish, seemingly unaware of my presence.

"You can only get black coffee with this one," I offer out of guilt.

Her ponytail whips around her as she turns to face me with wide brown eyes.

"Catalina," I say with a raspy voice.

Her nose scrunches at the sound of her full name. "What are you doing here, Lucas?"

"*Luke*," I emphasize with a smile before motioning toward my scrubs. "Isn't it obvious?"

"I thought Aiden was supposed to be working tonight."

"He was, but something came up. I think he mentioned an issue with the wedding cake?"

Her lips form an O.

"What are *you* doing here?" My gaze flickers over her scrubs. The cheery holiday pattern fabric isn't one I'd associate with her, but then again, my preference for basic dark-colored scrubs isn't reflective of my personality either. The only holiday cheer I'm spreading lately is a request for every patient to get the flu shot, so who am I to talk?

Catalina fiddles with the plastic clip of her ID badge, which is shaped and painted to resemble a snowman. "I'm filling in for someone who went on leave."

"For how long?"

"A month."

My surprise must be written across my face because she asks, "What?"

"I'm surprised is all."

"Why?"

"I thought you were popping in for the dress fitting and heading back to wherever you were needed next." Her hanging out here for a whole month is practically unheard of.

According to Aiden, Catalina was a travel nurse long before they started dating, which was one of the reasons it took him a while to realize he liked her more as a friend than a girlfriend.

She rocks back on her sneakers. "Between all the costs of the holidays and the wedding, it made more sense to stay put and get a job here."

I nod. "Got it. And how's it going living with your parents

again?"

"About as pleasant as an appendicitis."

"Pre- or post-op?"

"Is postmortem an option?"

I choke on a laugh. "Sounds wonderful."

"Tell me about it. Did I mention my mom is your biggest hype woman?"

I hide my wince. At first, it was nice to be acknowledged by Mrs. Martinez, but there is such a thing as killing someone with kindness, and I'm practically suffocating beneath hers.

I rub the back of my neck. "I assumed she was a fan of mine."

"Have you met someone who isn't?"

Yeah. You.

I wasn't born in Lake Wisteria, but I've lived here for the last year, so I've heard quite a bit about Catalina's…personality. I'm not put off by it in the slightest though.

If anything, I find her constantly pushing people away to be entertaining, given who her mother and sister are.

She interrupts my thoughts by asking, "Which button do I press?"

"Bottom left."

She tries again, but it doesn't work.

"Here. Let me try." I bang against the side of the machine, earning an amused huff from her.

"What?" I look down and find her *smiling*. It's small, but my heart trips over itself for a moment.

She shakes her head. "Men."

"That's a sexist statement. Perhaps I should report you to

HR for inappropriate workplace behavior."

"I'm sure they'll recognize your name when I place a complaint about you for checking out my ass."

"I... You..."

Her head tilts.

"How did you even see me?" My question comes out as a hiss.

"I could *feel* it."

"Hm." I cross my arms, earning a quick look from her that leaves her cheeks a bit flushed.

She clears her throat and returns her attention to the machine. "I was just pointing out that your first solution was to bang on the machine, so you're not doing your gender any favors here."

Oh.

The machine's menu screen glitches before prompting to pay again, earning a curse from Catalina. "It stole my money."

"Wouldn't be the first time that's happened." I've struggled with the same issue on a few occasions, which maintenance has yet to fix.

Before Catalina has a chance to tap her card against the machine, I pull mine out.

"What are you doing?" She reaches for my arm. Her fingers graze my bicep, sending a lick of heat over my skin.

The machine reads my chip with a beep.

"No!" Her nails dig into my skin.

"Should I add *unsolicited groping* to your report?"

She lets me go in a rush before glaring.

I tuck my card back in my wallet while the machine whirs

to life. "Relax. It's a cup of coffee. Not dinner and a movie."

"Thank you." She sighs as coffee starts filling the Styrofoam cup.

"Least I could do after what I said at lunch the other day."

And just like that, her body language changes. It's subtle, but obvious to anyone who cares enough to pay attention.

Catalina stares at the quarter-filled coffee cup, most likely willing the machine to go faster, but unfortunately, it always takes its sweet time. She even wraps her hand around the cup as if she plans on bolting the moment it lets out the final drop.

For some reason, I'm not ready for the conversation to come to an end. Now that I come to think of it, this might be the most time we've spent talking without her finding a way to escape the conversation, so maybe that's why I don't want her to run away.

"I'm sure your sister is happy you're here," I say to break the unbearable silence. I'm not the kind of person who enjoys them because it reminds me of too many days spent alone, wishing for someone to keep me company since my parents were too busy to do so themselves.

"Mm," she replies, not giving me much to work with.

Little does she know, I was an only child who had three imaginary friends while growing up, so I know plenty about keeping a conversation going.

"I'm shocked to see you wearing something other than black," I joke.

She turns to face me again, this time with a frown. She gives my outfit a bored once-over, although I catch her lingering on my arms for a little longer than necessary.

Okay. Clearly, she might dislike me as a person, but my body is a different story.

Catalina looks me in the eyes. "You're one to talk when you're dressed like the grim reaper."

"There are way too many bodily fluids in an ER to be dressed in anything *but* navy or black."

Her lips twitch, the edges threatening to curl at the corners, but she covers it up by clamping her mouth shut.

Getting that kind of rare reaction out of her makes me want to do it again, but before I take advantage of the opportunity, she stuns me by speaking.

"Not going to lie. You seemed like the type of guy who would wear his white coat everywhere he goes."

"I take personal offense to that statement."

"Good," she replies dryly, and I swear this girl makes me want to laugh without purposefully trying to.

"For your information, I prefer to keep my dry cleaning bills to a minimum."

"Is this your casual way of telling me you're broke?"

"I prefer the term *fiscally conservative.*" My comment earns the best kind of laugh.

My eyes widen. "Did you just…"

"*No.*"

"Whoa. I didn't think your internal software was capable of such a sound. Are you malfunctioning? Is there a 1-800 number I can call to get you help?"

She tries to glare, but it lacks the usual punch, given her eyes are sparkling with amusement. "Are you always this—"

"Charming?"

"Annoying. Seriously, it's like three a.m. Can you just not be like this right now?"

"Three a.m.? The night is still young then."

"Speak for yourself." On cue, she yawns, and damn if I don't find the way her face scrunches up to be cute.

Fuck. I think my best friend's ex-girlfriend is *cute*? That can be problematic, but then again, he is about to marry her sister, so who is he to judge? Aiden might even be a bit relieved given the couple of worried conversations I've overheard him having with Gabriela about Catalina, although I'm not sure the woman standing in front of me would share the same relief.

The machine chirps behind her. She grabs the Styrofoam cup, and her eyes close as she takes a sip. Instantly, her nose twitches and her forehead wrinkles with distaste.

"Tastes like shit, doesn't it?"

"God. That's awful." She coughs.

"Stick around long enough and you'll get used to it."

"Yeah, no. Not going to happen." She stares at her cup like it is laced with poison.

Honestly, given the distinct aftertaste, it might very well be.

I drain the rest of my drink and toss my empty cup in the trash. "Trust me when I say this is the best machine in the whole place."

"Really?"

"Yup. I've tested them all multiple times."

"Have you thought to put in a maintenance request?"

"Yeah, but no one has done anything about it, so I wouldn't hold my breath."

Her mouth opens, but my phone buzzes with a new message requesting my help in the ER before she has a chance to speak.

"I've gotta go," I say with a hint of reluctance.

"See you around." She lifts her cup. "And thanks for the shittiest coffee I've ever had."

"I owe you a better one."

She turns toward the direction of the NICU, but not before I see the small smile tugging at her lips.

Tonight, I didn't only make Catalina Martinez laugh, but smile *twice*, and I'll be damned because I'm already looking forward to when I can do it again.

shake it before
you taste it

CHAPTER FIVE

Catalina

'**ve** successfully been able to avoid my mother and her incessant request for my maid-of-honor speech for the last two days. Thankfully, by the time I crawl out of bed, she is already retiring to her room for the evening, claiming she has a headache after spending the day helping my sister figure out who can bake her a cake at the last minute for her wedding.

While eating a bowl of leftovers my dad saved for me, I check my phone for new messages. I'm not the most outgoing person, but I connected with a few nurses back in college who have refused to let me forget about them. Monica, Nancy, and Winny even created a group chat where we can catch up on everyone's lives, send the latest celebrity gossip, and share any job openings.

Last year, I got lucky that my agency set me up with a job at Monica's hospital, so I flew out to California and spent two months working and hanging out with her. I shelled out for a nice little spot close to the beach, and I swear it was one of the best subleases I've ever stayed in.

The Work Wives group chat, which was founded and named by Monica back when we were nursing students, is alive and well this evening after I mentioned my agency setting me up with another job opportunity in Los Angeles as soon as my sister gets married.

NANCY

What will it take for you to request a job near me?

MONICA

Shall I suggest moving somewhere more appealing?

NANCY

What's wrong with Arkansas?

MONICA

The fact that it isn't California.

WINNY

I hear Colorado is the new Cali.

MONICA

According to whom? The people who had to move out of LA because it was too expensive?

NANCY

Careful, Monica. Your privilege is showing.

MONICA

My privilege? Come visit my studio apartment and we will see about that.

NANCY

Speaking of convincing Catalina to come visit, I have a mansion.

MONICA

Yeah because it's ARKANSAS.

I fight a laugh as I respond.

ME

Wish I could see you all soon, but I'm staying in Lake Wisteria for the month.

MONICA

WHAT?

NANCY

Since when?

WINNY

And you planned on telling us this news when exactly...?

ME

I just agreed to take the job a couple of weeks ago.

ME

Seemed easier to stay put and help my sister with anything she might need for the wedding.

NANCY

You're a good sister.

ME

The bar is low.

NANCY

Just don't show up to her wedding hungover and you'll be loads better than me.

WINNY

And don't sleep with the best man.

NANCY

I forgot that happened! I must've wiped that traumatic memory from my brain, but thanks for the reminder.

An uncomfortable tightness forms in my chest when I consider the best man in my sister's wedding.

It's bad enough that I once dated the groom, even though we never slept together, but to possibly be interested in his best man, too? Worst idea ever.

A one-time fling to get Luke out of my system would only lead to more trouble than it's worth, and any residual awkwardness that'll occur afterward is reason enough to steer clear of him. Acting on a fleeting attraction would only further complicate an already sticky situation between Gabriela, Aiden, and me, so I'd rather keep my head down and make it through the month without any mistakes or unnecessary drama.

ME

> I already dated the groom, so I'll pass on the best man.

Later that night, once I return home after helping my sister finalize the seating chart for the wedding, I try working on my maid of honor speech. I only make it through a single sentence when a new message from an unknown number pops up on my phone.

UNKNOWN NUMBER

Hey.

I'm about to report the message as spam before a new one pops up with a photo of a Styrofoam cup I recognize all too well from the hospital.

UNKNOWN NUMBER

If I die tonight, please let them know I hated every sip of this.

My lips twitch as I save Luke's contact information incorrectly, solely because it makes me laugh.

I spend the next five minutes considering if I should answer him or not before reminding myself that it would be rude to snub my future brother-in-law's best friend.

ME

> If you end up dying, I *almost* feel bad for being the last person you text.

LUCAS

Some might consider that a
form of flattery.

ME

What's the antonym of that?

LUCAS

Fuck if I know. I'm a doctor, not a
thesaurus.

I hate that he's funny. It would be a hell of a lot easier to ignore him if he wasn't actively trying to not only talk to me but make me laugh too.

I come to my senses, and I'm about to exit the chat when another text shows up.

LUCAS

I'm about this close to buying an
espresso machine for the first-
floor break room.

He includes an emoji of two fingers pinched together with only a hair of space between them.

Because I can't seem to control myself tonight, I reply back.

ME

Given the number of nights
you spend there in a single
week, I highly suggest it.

LUCAS

Nurse's orders?

I find my lips curling at the corners.

ME

You're the doctor, so I'll defer to you.

LUCAS

Deferring to me might be hot in the bedroom, but not in real life.

And now I'm thinking about Luke in a completely different setting as he hovers over me, leaving a trail of kisses down my neck before—

My phone buzzes in my hand, killing the fantasy with a single message.

LUCAS

That was inappropriate.

ME

Extremely.

Talking is one thing, but flirting? A recipe for disaster to say the least.

LUCAS

Point is I don't know everything.

LUCAS

In fact, between us, I google symptoms and drug doses on a weekly basis.

ME

I think I now understand why you don't wear your white coat.

He follows up with a trio of question marks.

> **ME**
> Because you're an imposter.

LUCAS
Do you think that would
be probable cause for the
government to forgive my
student loan debt?

> **ME**
> I hear those get passed on
> to family members when
> you die, so I think not.

LUCAS
In that case, bottoms up.

He includes a coffee cup emoji, followed by a skull with
crossbones.

Talking to Luke has become...easy. He has this natural
charm that makes me want to keep the conversation going,
which in itself is a miracle because I'm always looking for the
easiest opportunity to see myself out of them.

Instead of letting our text thread die with his last message,
I spend a few minutes searching for the espresso machine
Winny bought herself for Christmas last year and send him
the link. It's one that uses pods that can be ordered online or
purchased at a mall thirty minutes away.

LUCAS
Serious question. If I invest in
this costly machine, would you
come visit me in the first-floor
break room?

> **ME**
> You? No.

> **ME**
> The machine? Absolutely.

The dots appear and disappear twice before his next message comes through.

> **LUCAS**
> Favorite flavor?

> **ME**
> Hazelnut.

> **LUCAS**
> Your wish is my command.

Luke texts me multiple times, but I keep my replies to a minimum of fifteen characters or less. It's easy to erect a wall, especially when I consider how a single conversation with him made me smile and laugh in a way I haven't done with a man in a long time.

Keeping my distance is in everyone's best interest. Things with Gaby and me are tense as it is, so the last thing I need to do is add another complicated layer to our family situation by becoming involved with the one person I will never be able to avoid.

Fate must be on my side because Luke and I don't run into each other at work for the next few days. After drinking a particularly watery cup of coffee from the machine, I almost texted him to check on the status of his espresso machine, but I deleted my message before I gained the nerve to hit send.

I should keep to myself during my time in Lake Wisteria. It's not like I plan on sticking around past January 1st, so it's best for me to avoid complicating matters by showing interest in my future brother-in-law's best friend. That title automatically would turn a one-night stand into a one-night mistake I'd have to face every time Gaby and Aiden decide to bring us all together.

Yet no matter how many times I've told myself that this past week, I'm reminded of Luke every time I pass by that disgusting coffee machine, and the urge to reach out to him becomes stronger.

Thinking about Luke in any capacity makes me... confused. After spending the last two years since Aiden and I broke up disliking him, I'm not sure what to make of my growing fascination, and I find myself thinking about him on more than one occasion.

So, when my sister invites me to join her and Aiden at the Lake Wist-mas Holiday Extravaganza that weekend, I jump at the opportunity to get out of the house and distract myself. In my desperation, I didn't truly consider what it would be like to spend an extended amount of time with my ex-boyfriend and my sister.

Before I started dating Aiden, Gaby and I were closer than ever, but now our relationship feels strained in a way that makes me anxious. I'm hoping this month can help us move past the awkwardness, but that doesn't mean it's easy.

I love my hometown, but I've made a point to find jobs that

take me as far from Lake Wisteria as possible, especially during the holidays. Given my mom's side hustle of selling bottles of my family's famous *coquito*, there was no way she and my dad could take time to visit.

Before the whole Aiden situation, Gabriela would alternate each year between spending Christmas with me and our family, but luckily for her, this year we can spend every single second of the holiday season together, starting with today's block party in the town square.

"I'm so happy you're here!" Gabriela claps her mittened hands together like she always did when we were little.

"Really?"

She snorts. "Yes, really. Is that so hard to believe?"

I stay quiet.

"Okay. What's going on?" She nudges me.

"Nothing," I say a little too quickly.

"Is it because of..." She tips her head in Aiden's direction.

"No." I emphasize.

Some tension bleeds away from her shoulders. "Oh. Good."

"I just feel bad."

"About what?"

"How weird things have gotten between us."

Her eyes soften. "Well, things are a little..."

"Awkward?"

A puff of warm air escapes her mouth from her soft chuckle. "Yes. Exactly."

"I hate it."

"Same." She ropes an arm around me. "How do we fix it?"

"I don't know." It's not like we haven't put any effort into our relationship, but no matter how hard we try, there is this lingering awkwardness.

Is it because of Gaby and Aiden, or does it have something to do with you?

A tightness in my chest makes breathing difficult. All this time, I thought my issue had more to do with Gaby and Aiden's relationship, but maybe my insecurity about never finding love is the real issue. Maybe I haven't been tense about Aiden and Gaby per se, but rather the loneliness that always hits me whenever I spend time with a couple that reminds me of what I don't have.

How will you ever find love when you find every reason to keep your walls up?

"Can we agree to never let a man get between us?" My sister asks, interrupting my spiral.

I clear my head with a quick shake. "Absolutely. Maybe I'll cut my losses and swear off men forever."

Gaby hip-checks me. "Let's not go to that extreme."

"I don't know. What's so great about them anyway?"

"I'll pretend you didn't just say that." Aiden tosses an arm around my sister's shoulder.

"Good," I say with a roll of my eyes while my sister giggles.

God, their love is so damn sweet, I'm instantly nauseated. Thankfully, the lights around us blink out, and everyone quiets as the mayor starts the countdown.

"Five…" the crowd gathered around us chants. "Four… three…two…one."

Everyone *oohs* and *ahs* as the forty-foot tree is lit.

My sister stares up at it like a kid opening their presents

on Christmas morning, and even I find myself entranced for a moment by all the twinkling lights. Despite the chilly air hitting us, a warmth spreads through my body as I remember the countless Christmas seasons we stood here, Gabriela holding my hand while Mami and Papi had their arms wrapped around each other.

Gabriela breaks the moment with an excited clap as she turns to face Aiden and me. "So, what do we want to do first? Sleigh ride through the town? Hot cocoa by the fire? S'mores?"

"Whatever you want." Aiden tucks my sister into his side to protect her from the wind coming off the lake while I'm stuck blowing on my mitten-covered hands to feel something other than the early signs of frostbite.

You won't be alone forever, I tell myself. *Just for now.*

"Should we go ice skating?" Gabriela's eyes light up.

I remember the last time I sprained my ankle and wince. "Um. I might pass on that one, but you should do it if you want."

"Actually, I think I know the perfect activity." Gabriela grins.

I decide to trust my sister and hope for the best. "Lead the way."

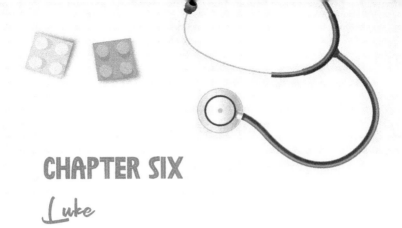

CHAPTER SIX

Luke

Aiden and I have kept a healthy competition going ever since we were first years in medical school. Without him and his annoying habit of betting on everything, I'm not sure I would've made it past the massive purge that takes place halfway through the first fall semester when people realize their dream of becoming a doctor was better left unexplored.

Since then, Aiden and I have found different ways to keep our rivalry going: sledding, snowball fights, pond hockey, ice skating. The list is endless, including us agreeing to participate in tonight's gingerbread house competition. When he mentioned the idea weeks ago, I told him I would be there, prepped and ready to kick his ass.

I never thought to check with him if Catalina would be joining us, mostly because I wouldn't mind if she does. Maybe that in itself would signal to my best friend that something is different between us because I've made a habit of doing otherwise. But if he's noticed, he hasn't asked why.

When I arrive at the tent that smells of gingerbread cookies and freshly made icing, Aiden, Gabriela, and Catalina all look at me like I've lost my mind.

"Did you seriously bring a level?" Aiden gapes at the tool in my left hand.

"You have no right to judge me here." Aiden has gone above and beyond in the past to win our bets, including taking private vocal lessons to beat me in a fundraiser karaoke competition, so he shouldn't talk.

Catalina, who is dressed in a jade green sweater that complements her golden skin and brown eyes, peeks over at the Ziploc full of supplies in my right hand. "Are those tongue depressors?"

"Yes, and if you report me to HR for copping supplies, I'll deny it until my dying breath."

Her tightly pressed lips are slowly curling at the corners. I swear I'm becoming obsessed with the idea of getting this girl to smile, even if it never lasts longer than a few seconds.

Her brow arches. "And the cotton balls?"

"Strictly for decor purposes."

"Of course." She glances away as if it could hide that amused sparkle in her eyes. I'm tempted to tug on the red velvet bow clipped to the back of her head to gain her attention again, but I refrain from the childish idea.

Gabriela looks over at Aiden and announces, "You're so going to lose."

He pulls her into his side. "Have a little faith in your fiancé."

"You need a miracle is more like it," Catalina grumbles under her breath, stroking my ego without even knowing it.

"Should we even bother trying?" Gabriela asks her sister.

She shrugs. "Probably not."

"What if we let the boys have their silly competition while we go check out—"

"Don't go," Aiden cuts her off. "We can make things interesting and split up into teams."

Wait. What? Never in all the years we have been friends has Aiden pulled a stunt like this, and I'm not sure how to process it. Teams? This man once gave me shit for using an ankle brace during a one-on-one basketball match, and now he wants to bring in reinforcements?

He looks over at me. "What do you say?"

"Couldn't think of a better idea." *To get myself in trouble.* Because I know exactly who my teammate is going to be.

With all the shifts Aiden and I have been pulling at the hospital lately, I haven't had an opportunity to talk to him about my growing interest in his ex-girlfriend. While I doubt he would give me much grief about it, I still feel some residual guilt from flirting with Catalina. Since my new espresso machine hasn't arrived yet, I've suffered through drinking from the worst coffee machine on the haunted third floor instead of taking a chance on us having another run-in near the NICU ward.

"You want to work in teams?" Catalina's lips purse, and for a moment, I wonder if she will be the one to save us all.

Feel free to say no. You won't hear me complaining.

Aiden smiles. "Me and your sister versus you and Luke the

Leveler over here."

Catalina might swallow her laugh, but Gabriela doesn't stop from unleashing a cackle.

"What do you say?" He wraps his arms around Gabriela's waist and kisses her cheek. "Wanna help me wipe the floor with them?"

"I'd love nothing more." She grins.

I expect Catalina to protest the idea, but she surprises me by saying, "The only thing you'll be wiping is that smile off your face when we win."

Well, shit. I shouldn't be turned on by the scary look on her face, but the devious smirk does something for me.

It's called a dopamine rush, and you of all people know those can become addictive.

She tilts her head back to look up at me. "We better not lose to them."

"Please. I did not watch three hours of gingerbread house tutorials for nothing."

"Seriously?" The awe in her voice makes my chest puff out.

"Are you impressed?"

"Horrified is more like it. Do you have nothing better to do with your free time?"

"Not particularly, no. It was either that or start a new LEGO set, and Aiden told me we didn't have the space for another one until he moves out."

"LEGOs?"

"Yes?" I ask with a hint of apprehension.

"Hm."

"Do you have something against them?" I pretend not to

notice the way Aiden and Gabriela whisper to each other while I am talking.

"Nope," she says with flushed cheeks.

Gabriela grins. "My sister loves building those."

Catalina's eyes widen.

"Is that right?" I smile.

She tenses beside me. "*Loved*. As in past tense."

"What changed?"

"I grew up."

Burn, Aiden mouths before covering his smile with the back of his fist.

Asshole. "That's a shame that adulthood killed your ability to have fun."

Her cheeks flush. "I know how to have fun."

"I'll believe it when I see it."

Her eyes narrow, and her lips part, only for her to be cut off by an announcement.

"Last call for gingerbread pieces before we run out."

And like that, my opportunity to learn more about Catalina and her love for LEGOs is stolen away all too soon.

"I refuse to be made fun of for using this." Catalina pushes the mini level in my direction.

I grab it from her and assess the angle of the slowly drooping roof. "There's no place for pride here."

"Trust me. I learned that lesson once I saw you refer to your phone for notes."

"I spent time compiling tips and tricks for a reason." And

that reason is slipping through my fingers as a supporting wall begins to sag.

She hits me with an exasperated look. I sneak a quick glance in Aiden and Gabriela's direction, where their gingerbread house is not only standing upright, but looking a lot more put together than ours.

Great. If Aiden wins this, I won't hear the end of it.

"Fuck." I curse when both pieces of our roof slide further apart.

"This is supposed to be fun, they said. Just a friendly competition, they said," she mutters quietly to herself beside me.

On cue, Aiden and Gabriela laugh when the walls of their house cave in.

"Whoops," he says before kissing the tips of Gabriela's icing-covered fingers.

It didn't hit me until now that Aiden never gave a damn about a stupid competition. All he wanted was to have fun with his future wife, while I've been drilling Catalina with directions for the last twenty minutes.

Because this really had nothing to do with a bet at all, did it?

I screw my eyes shut.

My parents were the type to turn everything into a competition between myself and the always-rising bar they wanted me to hit. Their expectations only got worse over the years because they needed me to be the very best at everything.

I had to be the top student and make the most friends. Had to find the perfect balance between a full social calendar, extracurricular activities, and an overwhelming academic load because the only thing that mattered was having a competitive college application. Then, once I got a full ride to the undergrad school of *their* choice like they had hoped, it was all about medical school and how to build myself up to be one of the most sought-after candidates.

I've spent my whole life competing against others, and while it helped me get where I am now, it's time to let it go.

Clearly Aiden doesn't care anyway, so why should I?

One of the gingerbread walls falls when Catalina tries to glue a gumdrop to the window, and she winces.

"Sorry." She scrambles to grab the bag of icing. "I'll fix it."

"It's okay." I clasp her wrist to stop her. Small goose bumps spread across her skin, and I find myself brushing my thumb over the curve of her wrist before reluctantly letting go.

She stares at me with wide eyes. "You just spent the last ten minutes creating interior support beams with tongue depressors and you think *this* is fine?" She motions toward the rubble pile of gingerbread pieces.

My guardian angel must be a comedian, because the last two walls standing fall in quick succession.

I shrug. "It's just a gingerbread house."

"What happened to pride?"

"Turns out I was mistaking it for male fragility."

She clamps a hand over her mouth to stifle her laugh, and I wish she hadn't gone out of her way to stop us all from hearing the sound.

"Does that mean you forfeit?" Aiden asks with a cocked brow.

I grab a piece of gingerbread that was meant to be the door

and take a bite. "Hell yes."

Catalina slumps against the table. "Thank God. That was more stressful than building a five-thousand-piece LEGO set."

"I take it you haven't tried to build the Galactic Command Base yet?" I ask with a smile.

"By myself? Hell no. It would take me years to finish without any help."

That's the exact reason why I haven't bothered buying it either. But maybe…

You need to talk to Aiden first.

First thing tomorrow, I plan on having a conversation with him about Catalina because there's no way I can continue pretending I don't like her company. It might not lead to anything more than friendship, but I'm okay with that.

Then why does your chest feel tight all of a sudden?

Because I can be friends with Catalina, but that won't stop me from being attracted to her.

Maybe if you befriend her, all this will fade over time.

Maybe it will. Maybe it won't. But I know one thing for certain. Come January first, she is leaving, so I only have three weeks to figure it all out.

I think I know the perfect way to start, so I only hope she agrees.

CHAPTER SEVEN

Luke

I go to sleep with a few thoughts on my mind about Catalina and seven hundred dollars less in my bank account and wake up with a new purpose.

I exit my room to find Aiden dressed in his work scrubs, making pancakes at four p.m. "Thank God your wedding is later in the day."

His reply is cut off by his yawn. "No way in hell are we getting up before noon. As the groom, I forbid it."

I take a seat at our kitchen counter and brush a hand through my ruffled hair. Our apartment is outdated but clean, and we even have a few picture frames hanging on the walls thanks to Gaby, although we haven't bothered replacing the generic stock photos that came with them.

If it weren't for Gaby strong-arming us into buying a small Christmas tree from the local farm and helping us pick out the most basic ornaments, our only holiday decor would've been a snowflake blanket that remains on our couch year-round, and a pair of matching stockings Aiden and I bought during a post-holiday clearance sale back when we were in med school. They were the only ones that had our initials on them, most likely because they have the ugliest plaid pattern I've ever seen. We like the memory enough to keep them, although Gaby seems eager to replace them for us.

Aiden serves me the first pancake from the batch. I think it's supposed to resemble a snowman based on the batter design, but I don't bother asking. It might be thin, brown on the edges, and suffering from a bulky center, but I'm too hungry to care as I take a massive bite.

"Thanks," I say after sipping on some water.

"No problem."

"You're the best roommate ever."

"Speaking of roommates…"

Oh no.

"Have you found a new one yet?" he asks while adding some batter to the pan in a shape that looks more like an obtuse triangle than a Christmas tree.

"Nope."

"This might be the first time I've ever seen you procrastinate with anything."

"Don't google what's wrong with me. According to WebMD, I'm probably dying."

He chuckles under his breath. "You can't keep putting this off forever."

"No, but I can put it off for *now*."

Once he gets married, Aiden will be moving in with Gaby,

and I will either have to find a roommate to take over Aiden's part of the lease or accept that I will have to live alone. I've avoided the task, both because of work and since I'm not sure what I want to do. Finding a roommate is going to be a pain in the ass, but living alone reminds me too much of my lonely childhood, so I'm struggling with analysis paralysis about the whole thing.

"We knew this would happen," he says with a sigh at the end.

"Yeah, well, I did hope we would be roommates for life, but then you had to go and fall in love with someone else like a complete cliché."

"One day, you'll be in a similar position." He has the absolute goofiest smile on his face.

"Maybe." I keep the hope out of my voice.

"You *do* want to get married, right?"

"Yes, but preferably to someone who wants to elope at the courthouse. Your wedding invoices give me second-hand hives."

"They're not *that* bad."

"Says the man paying eight grand for a videographer."

"Gaby says it'll be worth the cost when we show it to our future kids one day."

"I'm sure that's what she tells you to make you feel better."

He shoots me a half-hearted glare that makes me grin. Luckily, Aiden's job pays well, and Gaby makes good money as a certified public accountant in Lake Wisteria, or else I'd be concerned with the money they're spending on their special day.

"So…" He flips the pancake. "I wanted to ask you something."

"What?"

"Did anything seem off with Catalina yesterday?"

I stiffen before relaxing my muscles. "What do you mean?"

"I was just… I'm probably reading into things too much."

My heart, which was already stuttering a few seconds before, begins to pound harder in my chest. "Spit it out."

"I thought I noticed something between the two of you."

Fuck. My hand squeezes the fork I'm holding, but I loosen my grip before Aiden takes notice.

"Like what?" I ask with a rasp.

"Don't make fun of me for saying this."

I stare blankly at him.

"Just like…sparks?" He brushes his stubbled cheek.

I press my lips firmly together to stop myself from commenting, which earns me a glare.

"I'm being serious. She seemed…comfortable. With you, that is."

The thought sends a wave of warmth through me, feeding my confidence about the whole Catalina situation.

"I think she's warming up to me," I say with a light tone.

"Tell me about it. Just last week you were worried about a chopstick incident, and now you're hanging out at a holiday event without any issues?"

"I've been told on a few occasions that I'm hard to resist."

He stares at me with thinly pressed lips.

"What?"

He doesn't speak up right away, so my nerves get the best

of me as I say, "If you want to ask me something, do it before you kill me with suspense."

On the outside, I'm calm, cool, and charming, but on the inside, my emotions are all over the place.

"I don't know how to go about this, so I'm just going to give it to you straight and ask."

"Okay…"

"Are you into her?"

I look at him without blinking, and he does the same before breaking eye contact first.

"Shit. I wasn't sure if I was overthinking things, so Gaby insisted that I ask you."

"Gaby put you up to this?"

"Yes! She kept saying things were different between you two."

"If by different, she means her sister is no longer fantasizing about ways to escape a conversation with me, then I'd say yes. Things are progressing rather nicely between us."

His head tilts in quiet assessment.

"If you keep looking at me like a cadaver you want to dissect, I'm going to take my pancake and go so I can eat in peace."

His chest deflates with his sigh. "Sorry."

I'm the one who should be sorry since I'm the one interested in his ex-girlfriend.

I swallow the lump in my throat. "Now I have something to ask you."

"Yes?"

"Let's say, hypothetically speaking of course, I was

interested in your ex—"

He slaps the counter before pointing an accusatory finger at me. "I knew it!"

I can't tell whether he is mad or not. "This is strictly a hypothetical."

His lips curl at the corners.

Nope. Not mad.

The scent of something burning fills my nose, and Aiden rushes over to the stove. With a curse, he tosses the crispy pancake in the trash before pouring more batter in the pan.

"So, you're not angry?" I ask with slight uncertainty.

"Why on earth would I be mad about that?" He turns to face me with crossed arms.

"Well, Catalina is *your* ex."

"So? I'm in love with her sister. Plus, Catalina and I were hardly together. At least in that sense."

"You dated each other."

He casually lifts a shoulder. "And during that time, she was traveling around the country for work. We might have talked every day, but it was more platonic than anything else."

"Got it," I say with a note of finality to my tone.

He chuckles to himself.

I take a few more bites of my food before talking. "You really wouldn't be upset if I—I don't know. Talked to her more?"

He laughs to himself. "I swore I'd never say this aloud."

Now *that* makes me curious.

I place my elbows on the counter and lean forward. "What?"

"I always thought you two were better suited for each other."

"Really?" And he kept this to himself for exactly *how* long?

"Yeah. It's one of the reasons I broke up with her, but I never told her that of course. Especially since she didn't seem to like you very much once you met."

Oh shit. I thought the only reason Aiden called it off with Catalina was because he started being interested in her sister as more than a friend.

Aiden continues, "There were little things you said or did that always reminded me of her. That's probably why I took to being her friend so easily."

"How did you even become her friend?" Aiden might have told me once before, but I don't remember.

"You of all people know she isn't the kind of girl who lets people get too close, too fast."

"Tell me about it."

"It took me some time to wear her down, but she's a great girl who just needs people to take the time to get to know her."

"So I'm starting to realize," I say with a sigh.

"I will say that whoever earns her trust and loyalty better do everything possible to protect it or else they'll have to deal with me."

My last bite tastes like ash in my mouth. "Are you going to be an overbearing ex?"

"*Worse*. A protective brother-in-law."

"That's supposed to be worse?"

"Yup, because anyone who hurts Catalina is guaranteed to upset my future wife, which will instantly piss me off."

Based on the glint in his eye, I hope no one ever crosses Gaby's path.

"Watching you fall in love like this is fascinating," I say.

He shoots me a smile. "I look forward to saying the same thing to you one day."

"I never said I was falling in love with anyone."

"That's what we all say before it happens."

I blink twice, and he leans over the counter to clap me on the shoulder.

"Relax. Take it day by day and see what happens."

Famous last words.

*shake it before
you taste it*

CHAPTER EIGHT
Catalina

"I was hoping to catch you before you left for work."
My sister pops into my room and shuts the door
softly behind her.

I turn around. "What's up?"

"I wanted to talk to you about something I noticed at the
holiday block party."

"What?" My stomach drops.

"You and Luke."

"What about us?"

"You two were…"

"Just playing nice," I say a little too quickly.

She shoots me a look that sends my heart racing. "Cata."

My legs threaten to buckle, so I take a
seat at my old desk while my sister sits on
the edge of my bed. "Nothing is going on
between us."

A line appears between her
furrowed brows. "I saw the way you

were both looking at each other."

"And?"

"I'm worried."

"About what?"

Her eyes roll. "Come on. Anyone with a lick of common sense can pick up on your interest in each other."

I shake my head. "He's attractive, but that's all."

"I'm not dumb."

"And neither am I. Luke is the last person I should get involved with." The words tumble out of my mouth.

"Why?"

"Because he's Aiden's best friend."

She lets out a relieved breath. "Hence my worry."

I abandon my chair and take a seat beside her on the bed. "I'm not going to risk hooking up with him or something if that's what you're scared about."

"It's not." Her heavy breath fills the silence. "I just don't want to lose you again when it feels like I finally got you back," she whispers.

I blink a few times. "What? You never lost me."

"It sure felt like it for the last two years since Aiden and I started dating."

Guilt sinks its sharp claws into my chest. "Gaby..."

"I can't stand the thought of you avoiding me again, and I'm worried if you and Luke have a fling or something, then you'll find another reason to stay away."

"I'm not going to avoid you."

"Even if something were to happen between you and Luke?"

I reach for her hand and give it a squeeze. "Nothing is going to happen, but yes, no matter what happens, I promise to stick around."

She offers me a weak smile. "I'm sorry for freaking out. It's just that I could feel the connection between you two, and the what-if scenarios freaked me out."

Even more of a reason to steer clear of Luke.

Gabriela already has enough to worry about without me complicating matters by hooking up with her future husband's best man, and it's best I remember that.

I knew I wanted to become a NICU nurse when we visited my aunt in Puerto Rico after she gave birth to my cousin. We had originally planned for a fun trip to spend time with her and our family, but things changed after my aunt's hellish C-section and my cousin was rushed to the hospital's NICU floor.

It only took a few visits to the NICU for me to become fascinated by the nurses who were helping keep my baby cousin alive, and by the time he was finally discharged, I fell in love with the idea of saving lives like them. In my eyes, they were heroes, and despite the job's challenges, I haven't lost that idealistic view, although it's been tested plenty of times during the bad days.

Most people assume because I work with babies, I must be the happiest nurse around, but they don't see the darker side of the job. Managing feeding tubes and respirator devices that support many lives in the unit. Parents breaking down in front of the baby they desperately want to take home, blaming everyone under the sun, including themselves, for medical issues. All the lives I've seen snuffed out before they ever had a chance to really live, and the shattering of parents' hearts as they wanted to die with them.

Unfortunately, today might be one of the worst ones yet. I'm not sure if I'm struggling more because it's the holidays and I'm more sensitive to all the babies who may never get to make it to their next Christmas, but I find myself needing to take multiple breaks.

"You've got to do something." Debra, a mom I've spent the last week getting to know, clings to my snowman-themed scrubs. "There must be something else we can do. If money is an issue, we'll find a way to get it. Or if we need to take her to another hospital, then let's coordinate a transfer. We're willing to do whatever it takes."

My damn eyes water, betraying me.

"Please." Her voice cracks.

Debra's wife tries to pull her off me, but I shake my head and wrap my arms around her.

"I'm so sorry." I rub her back.

She trembles in my arms. "She's my baby."

"And you're her wonderful mom." I keep my tears from falling, but my heart weeps for the two mothers standing in front of me.

"Why, God? Why?" She lets go of me before turning to her wife.

Trish, who has been Debra's rock for the last month that their daughter has spent in the NICU, throws her arms around her wife and pulls her into an embrace. "I'm sorry, babe. I'm so fucking sorry."

"This isn't fair." Debra clutches Trish's shirt with a tight fist. "It was never supposed to be like this."

My chest feels like it might cave in on itself. Not wanting the two of them to see me break down, I turn and fiddle with their daughter's machines before my eyes land on the card at the front of her plastic-encapsulated bed.

Sarah Lynn, 3 lbs 4 ounces.

Her moms even brought a one-month-old sign from home and hung it on the front of her bed. It was meant to be used in happy photographs in their home as they created their first memories as a family, but now, it's a heartbreaking reminder of the life they could have had.

Sarah won't live to see her second month, no matter how hard her mothers cry or what kind of medical intervention we do to help her.

I brush my hand over the sign. A tear slips out despite my best efforts, and I motion for another nurse to take over for me. She rushes over, whispers a reassuring comment in my ear, and lets me know to take as much time as I need.

With my heart feeling like it might split in two, I exit the NICU and head toward the closest elevators. I don't care how cold it is or if I have a jacket. I *need* fresh air.

I pass by the shitty coffee machine. For a single moment, the ache in my chest lessens, only to return with a vengeance when I think of Luke finding me acting like this.

Go before someone sees you.

I hit the button with the downward arrow and wait. The elevator always takes a while due to patients being loaded and unloaded on each floor, so I suffer in silence as I wait.

Sarah Lynn.

Ana Lucia.

Luis Fernando.

The list of lives that have been lost during my time as a NICU nurse plays in my head, along with Debra's cries. I promised myself long ago that I would never forget the ones who didn't make it, and despite the list getting longer, I haven't yet.

I'm not sure how long I spend waiting for the elevator, but next thing I know, I'm wiping at my wet cheeks and cursing myself for having a breakdown in public.

I'm supposed to be the strong one. The person parents look to for help and support, yet here I am, crying my eyes out in a hallway where anyone can stumble upon me.

I turn away from the elevator, thinking I'm better off using the stairwell. Before I take a single step toward the door, the elevator opens with a *ding*.

"Catalina?"

My body turns to stone at the sound of Luke's voice.

Shit. Shit. Shit.

The illuminated exit light taunts me as I battle between making a run for it or turning to face Luke like an adult.

With a reluctant sigh and a quick swipe over my cheeks and underneath my nose, I do the latter. His brows rise as his gaze collides with mine, making the ache in my chest worse.

I can only imagine what I look like right now, so I steel my spine and slide my cold mask of indifference into place as I mentally prepare for whatever questions he will pepper me with.

When the elevator doors begin to close, he throws his arm out to stop them, but I don't step inside.

"Were you looking to go downstairs?" His question surprises me, not only because he predicted my next move, but also since he chose to overlook the fact that I was crying.

I nod because I don't trust my voice to not break.

He reaches over and presses a button. "I've got a better idea."

When I don't enter the elevator right away, he lets out a heavy breath. "If you don't want to be around anyone, that's fine. I completely understand."

"No," I say too quickly, catching me by surprise. Usually, I'm the first one to avoid others until I can get my emotions under control, but the idea of being alone makes me feel worse.

So Luke is your best option?

I glance up at him through tear-soaked lashes and am taken aback by how concerned he looks. It feels nice for someone to be worried about me for once rather than being the one to fuss over everyone else, and I soak it up, allowing the warmth of his gaze to erase the cold feeling of dread that was overwhelming me earlier.

He dips his head. "Then get in."

I don't need to be told twice. Anywhere seems better than here right now, so with a deep breath, I enter the elevator and hope for the best.

Turns out Luke's idea is far superior to mine. The sixth floor, which is nothing but a small rooftop patio with an ashtray and an empty planter that serves as a makeshift trash can, gives me enough space and privacy to properly breathe for the first time in hours. The smell of antiseptic still clings to my scrubs, skin, and hair, but the crisp air rolling off the lake clears my foggy head.

I lean against the ledge and shut my eyes, counting my breaths to keep my mind away from unpleasant thoughts.

Luke stands beside me, giving me some much-needed warmth as our sides press together. When he asks if I'm cold, I shake my head, although his gaze narrows at the goose bumps spreading across my arms.

No way in hell am I going to confess that the reaction is because of him, not the weather, so I stick to saying nothing at all. He does the same, which might be a first. Come to think of it, I don't remember him ever sitting in comfortable silence before—a fact I bluntly point out.

"I don't like long pauses," he answers after my rude comment.

"Why not?"

He takes a two-second pause before saying, "It reminds me of all the time I spent by myself as a kid."

His honesty is refreshing and downright commendable.

"Lucky you," I joke to lessen the tension in his jaw. "Some days I was begging Gabriela to shut up."

He chuckles. "I wish I had a sibling to pester."

"No doubt you would have driven them crazy."

"They would've come to appreciate my form of love."

"Like sibling Stockholm syndrome?"

"Precisely."

I find myself smiling for the first time since I started my shift, and it makes me feel all kinds of ways.

"What?" he asks with pinched brows.

I consider brushing off his question, but for some reason, I choose to be honest. "I feel guilty."

He nods. No pushing me to elaborate on what exactly I feel guilty about. No pestering me for answers I'm not ready to give. Nothing but the comfort of his presence as he stands beside me and looks out at the town. Christmas lights decorating the local businesses and houses twinkle in the distance, filling me with warmth and hope after spending the night sick with cold dread.

Luke shifting his weight distracts me from the view.

I fiddle with my snowman badge clip. "I don't want to keep you."

"Tonight's been painfully slow, so you're doing me a favor."

My lips turn up at the corners. "Am I?"

"Yup. I hate feeling useless."

"Must be that savior complex acting up again."

"Are you diagnosing me?" He turns to face me with a smile.

"I would never dare, Doctor Darling."

He beams. "Say that again."

I roll my eyes. "And feed your power trip? No thanks."

The sparkle in his eyes rivals the stars above us. "Please. At this rate, I will be begging for scraps of your attention."

"You call this begging?" My gaze flickers over his tall form. It takes me far more effort than it should to fake my disinterest, especially with the way he fills out his scrubs. "Consider me unimpressed."

"If you wanted me on my knees for the full effect, all you needed to do was ask."

His words are like magic, sending an image through my head of him doing just that. Except we wouldn't be on a roof, but rather, he would be on his knees, his hands reaching for my—

"By all means, feel free to share whatever thought is making you look at me like *that*."

My cheeks burn. Thankfully, the night sky shields him from noticing…or so I thought.

He cups my warm cheek, and I suck in a breath at the way my body lights up from a single brush of his thumb against my skin.

My instant response to his touch scares me, not due to feeling guilty over being attracted to Aiden's best man, but because I can't remember the last time someone made me feel so much in such a short span of time.

Maybe not ever.

I've noticed sparks of attraction before, but this seems like more. I can't put my finger on it, but I don't know many people who have made me feel the same way Luke does with a single look and a fleeting touch, and it *terrifies* me.

I don't have plans to stick around Lake Wisteria. Nor am I going to pursue a connection with someone who is tied to my sister and future brother-in-law and risk spending the rest of my life in an awkward situation when things don't work out. After today's conversation with my sister, I wouldn't have an option to do so even if I wanted to.

Despite wanting to stay put and bask in the way Luke looks at me, I take a big step back and wrap my arms around my torso.

His brows scrunch together, and his hand hangs in the air. "Catalina?"

"Thanks for showing me this place." I take another step closer to the stairwell that leads to the elevator.

"Where are you going?"

Far away from here.

I refuse to jeopardize the newfound peace between my sister and me by acting on our attraction. Desiring Luke is one thing, but I can't take it further than that and risk the awkwardness that is bound to occur if a temporary fling came to an end.

No matter how much he tempts me to do the complete opposite.

CHAPTER NINE

Luke

I fucked up. That much becomes clear after Catalina pulled away from me on the rooftop and threw her walls up higher than ever before.

I told myself I'd give her space, but I go against my better judgment and text her after my shift, needing to check if she is doing okay. Unlike all my other messages, she doesn't answer this one, which makes me feel worse.

I shouldn't have touched her the way I had. It was a bold move given our situation, but I couldn't resist wanting to comfort her—and look where that got me.

I'm not sure how to best navigate the situation, so I turn to Aiden for advice, only for him to involve Gaby, who happens to be hanging out in our apartment, helping pack up some of his belongings.

"What does he mean you're interested in my sister?" She shoots Aiden a pointed look after he stated the obvious a moment before.

Aiden salutes me from behind her back. *Good luck*, he mouths.

Bastard. "I like her."

"Since when?"

"It's a rather new development."

My soon-to-be ex-best friend snorts, and I'm tempted to smack him on the side of his head.

Gaby plants her hands on her hips. "So, it's nothing serious then."

"I never said that."

"As your best friend's future wife, I deserve to know what your intentions are with my sister."

"I'm not sure that's how it works."

She throws her arms up. "Luke!"

"What?"

"Stop being cryptic!"

"All right, fine. Yes, I'm interested in Catalina, and I already talked to Aiden about it, so it shouldn't be an issue if that's what you're worried about."

She curses under her breath.

"What?" I ask as my stomach drops.

"You should've spoken to me too."

"Why?"

Her gaze drops. "Because I just had a whole conversation with her about why she should stay away from you."

"Why would you do that?" Horror bleeds into my voice.

"Because I didn't think you seriously liked her!"

"Well, thanks for checking in with me before giving her another reason to stay away."

Gaby winces. "Sorry. Aiden hadn't talked to me about your conversation yet and I panicked after the gingerbread house thing. I feel like I'm just starting to get my sister back, and I'm worried that she would go back to avoiding me if you two... you know..."

"Hooked up?"

"Yes," she says with a groan.

"I'm not the kind of person that casually hooks up with people."

She avoids eye contact. "Yes, but Cata isn't like you."

I take a deep breath. "Noted." I'm not about to hold Catalina's history against her, so it doesn't matter.

"But she isn't completely against relationships." Aiden offers, as if I needed a reminder of their past.

Gaby pinches the bridge of her nose. "This is a mess."

"I'd say." I collapse onto the couch.

Gaby starts pacing the length of our living room. "If I had known you actually were interested in my sister—"

"You didn't exactly give me a chance to talk to you about it first."

"I'm sorry." She drops onto the sectional piece parallel to me.

"What am I supposed to do now?"

It takes Gaby a minute to speak up again. "I think I have an idea."

I beckon her to continue.

"My sister requires a certain kind of handling."

"Is she a package or a person?"

Gaby glares.

"Okay, okay. I'm listening."

She rubs her chin. "If you come off too strong, you'll scare her away for good."

"A little too late for that," Aiden whispers under his breath for all of us to hear.

I flip him off before asking, "What do you suggest?"

"Tell me what you have in mind first."

"Well, before this chat, I bought the Galactic Command Base LEGO set and planned on inviting her over to build it."

Both of their jaws drop.

"Is that a bad idea?"

"You bought a seven-hundred-dollar LEGO set for a first date?"

I rub the back of my neck. "Well, I wasn't going to tell her it's a date."

Aiden and Gabriela share a look.

"What?"

Aiden speaks first. "If you're inviting her over to your apartment to build a LEGO set together, then it's a date."

"Do you think she'll see it that way?"

Gaby looks up at the ceiling and mutters for help. "Yes."

"What are my chances of her agreeing?"

"Before the conversation I had with her? Maybe twenty percent."

"And now?"

She makes a face.

I drop my head back against the couch. "Fuck me."

Gaby frowns. "Let me help you. Please?"

Aiden nods aggressively behind her. *Yes*, he mouths. *Say*

yes.

"Sure."

Gaby's smile returns in full force. "Okay. But first I need to know when the set is being delivered."

I check my phone. "Tomorrow." Along with the espresso machine I plan on installing before my next shift.

"Perfect." Her smile is borderline concerning, but once she tells me her plan, I find myself wearing a similar expression.

"I'll talk to my sister and do some damage control, and Aiden will help you with the rest." Gaby rubs her hands together like an evil villain.

Looks like my odds of Catalina agreeing to come over just got a whole lot higher because with Gaby and Aiden helping me, she doesn't stand a chance of resisting.

shake it before you taste it

CHAPTER TEN
Catalina

I curse with frustration as I reread the opening sentence for my maid of honor speech. At this rate, I'll never have a speech written in time for Gabriela's wedding, and I will have no one to blame but myself and my inability to express myself.

A new text from my sister only adds to the growing sense of panic building inside me.

GABRIELA

Look at what Luke bought!

She attaches a photo of an unopened Galactic Command Base LEGO set. To say I'm shocked he purchased it is an understatement, especially after the conversation we had while making the gingerbread house.

I never told him this, but I've wanted to build that one ever since LEGO announced the addition to their collection. Whenever my sister mentioned wanting to buy it for me, I told her that I wasn't interested, which was partially true, but not the whole truth.

I wasn't interested because I didn't have anyone to build it *with*.

Knowing Gabriela, she would say it didn't matter. That I could build the set myself, but she is in a happy relationship and doesn't understand my struggle. How a hobby I didn't mind doing on my own became a reminder of not having anyone to enjoy it with, and I partially have social media to blame for ruining that activity for me.

I could only handle seeing so many videos of people building LEGOs with their significant others before I started associating my favorite hobby with crippling loneliness. Not to mention every time I visited the store, there was always one person in line buying a LEGO bouquet to build, which only made the feeling worse.

My phone buzzes in my hand.

GABRIELA

What do you think?

A lot of things, none of which I plan on sharing with you, I tell myself before typing out a reply.

ME

I can't believe he actually bought it.

GABRIELA

Me neither! Luke is kind of cheap.

> **ME**
>
> He prefers the term
> "fiscally conservative."

GABRIELA

It's cute that you come to his
defense.

Cute? Consider me surprised by that comment after our
last conversation.

I blow out a breath while writing out another message.

> **ME**
>
> What happened to waiting to
> buy it until Aiden moved out?

The dots appear and disappear twice before her next text
pops up.

GABRIELA

They compromised.

> **ME**
>
> On?

GABRIELA

Aiden wants to help build it.

I frown as I read her message twice.

> **ME**
>
> But Aiden hates LEGOs.

He used to tell me that his hands were too big, and his
attention span too short for a hobby like that, so why the
sudden change of heart?

GABRIELA

Maybe he wants to spend time
with Luke before he moves out?

GABRIELA

The two of them have been
acting all sentimental and extra
needy lately.

My mom calls my name from the kitchen, so I tuck my phone into my pocket and head toward the Christmas music playing down the hall. My smile widens as the singer croons about *mi burrito sabanero*, and it expands to its limit as I check out the messy counters covered with supplies and ingredients for my grandma's *coquito* recipe.

Both of my parents hang out by the stove, with my mom holding out a spoon for my dad to taste-test her latest batch of *coquito*.

Mami looks over her shoulder. "Oh good. You're awake."

My dad glances at me from across the kitchen. "You woke up just in time."

"What's up?"

"Can you hold the bottles for me while I pour?" he asks while my mom continues stirring the *coquito* mix in the pot.

My throat tightens as I nod. Empty glass bottles are lined up in a perfect row on the counter, with the one closest to the edge already set up with a funnel.

Mami leans forward to smell the mixture. "*Está casi listo.*"

"*Huele a los que hacía mi mamá.*" Dad's eyes twinkle as he kisses Mami's cheek.

The music. The *coquito*. The request to help my parents with a task that they always do together, reminding me of what I could have too—if I ever found the right person, that is.

The holidays always have a way of making people like me feel lonelier than usual, especially when we're constantly being bombarded with holiday movies, TV commercials, and endless books waxing on about love, family, and the meaning of Christmas.

Do you expect to meet someone special with the amount of traveling you do? It's hard enough to get into a routine, let alone fall in love. But when I think of permanently staying somewhere, I get cold feet. None of the places where I've worked felt quite right, but Lake Wisteria isn't an option either if I want to meet someone special. After all, I tried that with Aiden and look where it got me.

I turn toward the counter, shut my eyes, and take a deep breath. The smells remind me of years spent running around the kitchen with Gabriela, tugging on our parents' clothes while they worked in tandem to complete as many *coquito* orders as possible before Christmastime. My grandma had been selling the spiked holiday drinks long before we were born, so my parents have her operation down to a science.

A recipe card on the counter catches my eye, and with a shaky hand, I reach for it. The Martinez family's *coquito* recipe is written in my grandma's recognizable chicken scratch, along with her famous *shake it before you taste it* advice, which she wrote on every customer's thank you card.

My entire chest aches as I trace over the words in her familiar scrawl. She was a constant boisterous presence in our home after she moved to Lake Wisteria to live with us, and the holidays always make me miss her a little extra.

"Cata?" Mami asks from behind me.

I take a deep, cleansing breath. *"¿Qué?"*

"¿Estás bien?"

"Si." I carefully place the recipe card back on the counter facedown, so I no longer have to look at it, and get to work.

My mom might sense something is off, but thankfully, she doesn't ask about it.

Then why do you feel so heavy whenever you think about her not pushing to make sure you're okay?

Sometimes, I wish my mom would try a little harder with me, but instead, she always gives up at the first sign of adversity. With Gabriela, she bends over backward to be everything my sister needs and more, but when it comes to me, she seemed to have given up years ago, and in many ways, I did too.

"Gracias, mi hija." My dad releases me from his crushing hug before exiting the kitchen, leaving me all alone with my mom.

I wipe down the counter while she places a label on the final *coquito* bottle. The silence isn't awkward, but I find it stifling, and I'm desperate to escape back to my bedroom as quickly as possible.

"Cata?" my mom asks.

"¿Si?"

"Thank you for helping us today. Your dad's mom…" Mom struggles with the word. "She would have been so proud to see you helping us out. You know how much she loved making *coquito* for the town."

My mom's rare praise makes my throat feel thick with emotion. "You're welcome."

She stares down at the tile floor before looking up. "I know things were a bit tense last week, but I'm happy you came home for the holidays."

"You are?"

She looks surprised by my own shock. "Of course."

"Oh."

She leans back against the countertop. "I know we don't always see eye-to-eye on things, but you're still my daughter."

"Doesn't always feel that way," I say hesitantly.

Her brows pinch together. "Excuse me?"

"Nothing."

"No. Explain what you meant by that."

I motion to the space between us. "I know you prefer Gabriela over me."

Her eyes widen. "Why would you say that?"

"It's obvious that you wish I were different—"

"I *never* said that."

"You didn't need to. I can just tell."

A flush crawls up her neck. "How?"

"You act like everything I do annoys you."

"Me? I feel like *I'm* the one who always annoys *you*."

I blink twice. "What?"

"You've been pulling away from me for a while, and I don't know how to deal with it. It makes me feel like I failed you somehow. My mom"—she looks around the kitchen before her eyes land on the recipe card on the counter—"wasn't like your dad's mom. She wasn't good at talking about her feelings or giving me space to express myself." My mom's throat tightens with her swallow. "With your father, I've learned how to communicate over the years, but with you…I just don't know how." Her head drops forward.

My heart sinks into my chest. "Mami."

She looks up with glistening eyes. "I swore I wouldn't be like my mother. She wasn't very present in my life, so I promised to be the opposite, and I know that can come off as…"

"Suffocating," I answer honestly.

She glances away. "Yes."

"Overbearing."

"I guess so."

"Like I'm always disappointing you, even when I'm trying my best?"

She sniffles. "I'm sorry my actions made you feel that way."

I reach over and grab her hand. "I know you try in your own way."

She shakes her head. "But it isn't good enough."

"It's not that it isn't good, but it isn't what I need." Her face pales, so I scramble to express myself better. "At least not now. I want to feel like I can count on you to lift me up." *Rather than tear me down.*

"Tell me what else you need."

"Honestly?"

She nods. "Yes."

"I just want to feel like you see *me*. Like you appreciate who I am and all my differences because I'm never going to be like you and Gabriela, but that doesn't mean I don't feel left out."

She gives my hand a squeeze. "*Perdón, mi mijita.* I…I can try. I'm not going to get it right the first time, or the second, but I'm hoping I can do better for *you.*"

My mom and I may not agree on many things, but today, I feel more connected with her than ever.

It takes us a few minutes to collect ourselves, but once we do, I let her go and search for one of our favorite holiday songs on my phone.

My mom and I both finish cleaning up the kitchen while music plays from the portable speaker. When my mom plays one of my grandmother's favorite songs, I'm hit with an idea.

"Speaking of Abuela, you know what she would've loved?" I ask.

My mom stops sweeping the floor to look up at me. "*¿Qué?*"

"*Una parranda.*"

"How's the speech going?"

I jolt at the sound of my sister's voice behind me before slamming my notebook shut. "What are you doing here?"

"Mami wanted to go over a few wedding things, so I stopped by after work."

"Oh." I turn my office chair around to face her. "How's it going?"

"Good. I also thought it would also be a good time to apologize."

"To Mom? For what?"

"No." She shakes her head. "To *you.*" She drags my vanity stool across the room and takes a seat in front of me.

"But you haven't done anything wrong."

"Just let me get this out."

"Okay." I seal my mouth shut.

"I overreacted the other day and let my fears get the better of me."

I resist the urge to interrupt her.

"When everything went down between you, Aiden, and me, I felt like I gained a boyfriend but lost my sister."

I hold my hand out, and she places hers on top of mine before locking our fingers together.

She continues, "When I saw you and Luke hitting it off, at first, I was excited because I've always wanted you two to get along, but then reality sunk in, and I got worried about what could happen if you two *really* hit it off. If you get what I mean."

"I do, but I'm the last thing you should be worrying about."

"You're not a thing. You're my sister, and I care about your happiness, which is why I'm saying sorry."

"I appreciate the thought but—"

"But nothing. If our roles were reversed, you wouldn't want me to be unhappy, right?"

"Of course not, but this isn't the same—"

She interrupts me again. "Yes, it is. Your happiness is equally as important as mine."

"I am happy." I emphasize.

She hits me with a look that makes me feel like she doesn't entirely believe what I'm saying. "Does it make you happy to know that Luke bought the Galactic Command Base solely because he wanted to build it with you?"

My eyes widen.

"Or does it make you happy to hear that he talked to me about how he is interested in you?" she asks when I don't answer.

My heart skips a beat.

"That look right there is why you shouldn't stay away from Luke because of my irrational fears."

"They're not irrational." Especially not when I have the same ones.

"You're both adults who can handle your own shit, and you owe it to yourself to at least give him a shot, right? Even if it leads to nothing but awkward silence whenever you two hang out with us."

"Are you supposed to be convincing me to give him a chance or reminding me why I should stay away from him?"

She laughs. "I'm only giving you the worst-case scenario while hoping for the best."

"And what's the best?"

She shoots me a smile. "That's up to you to decide."

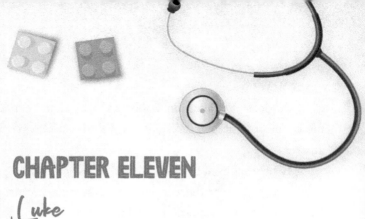

CHAPTER ELEVEN

Luke

When Gaby's first idea of texting Catalina about the Galactic Command Base LEGO set didn't lead to promising results, seeing as Catalina didn't take the bait, Aiden's fiancée decided to kick things up a notch by having a conversation with her sister and inviting her over for dinner at our place. She used Aiden's cooking as an incentive, and Catalina agreed just like we thought she would.

I've never met a single person who could say no to a meal prepared by Aiden because he is one of the best cooks around. After having him help me meal-prep for the last year, I'll be stuck fending for myself in the kitchen once he moves out, which is one of the many reasons why I'll miss sharing a place with him.

Think happy thoughts, I tell myself while helping Aiden wrap up the finishing touches on his mom's lasagna recipe.

"That smells so good." Gaby's eyes light up at the casserole dish

being placed on the small, round table in our makeshift dining room. The cheese is a perfect shade of golden yellow while the sauce bubbles beneath the surface, making my mouth water.

Aiden takes a photo of his handiwork. "My mom always said the way to a woman's heart is through her stomach."

"Thank God I can bake then, or else I'd be screwed," I say, thinking of when he put me in charge of the Thanksgiving side dishes last month and I failed miserably.

He gives me a once-over. "I mean, you're not the *worst* cook out there."

"Thanks, man. I appreciate the honesty."

He smiles. "If things with Catalina go well, maybe she can teach you a thing or two."

"Oh, yes. My sister's *mofongo* is just...*divina*," Gaby says the word with a soft sigh that can barely be heard over the holiday music streaming out of the portable speaker on the kitchen counter.

Gaby took it upon herself to add some additional decorations to our apartment today, including hanging multicolored lights along the top of our wall-length bookshelf, searching our closets for a nativity set that her mother bought for Aiden, and finding a place for it on a shelf, and setting the table with a holiday-themed tablecloth, placemats, and dinnerware.

Speaking of Catalina, the buzzer by our front door goes off, and Aiden presses the button to let her into our small walk-up. My heart picks up speed at the thought of Catalina seeing our place for the first time. I quickly scan the room again, double-checking to make sure that everything is in order.

Gaby rushes to open the door, acting as if she didn't see

her sister a few hours ago while Aiden and I hang back in the breakfast nook.

"Come on in." Gaby grabs Catalina's hand and pulls her inside.

Catalina glances around our apartment and the growing pile of moving boxes by the front door before looking over at Aiden and me. Her eyes narrow when they connect with mine, and for a brief moment, I wonder if this was a terrible plan.

Now you're questioning it? I shift my weight with nervous anticipation.

"Aiden made your favorite!" Gaby drags Catalina further into the apartment before shutting the front door behind her.

"And I helped," I tack on, earning another wary glance from Catalina.

"By *helped* he means taste-tested the sauce." Aiden's grin expands.

I shrug. "It's tough work but someone has to do it."

Catalina's eyes roll as she walks up to Aiden and greets him by pressing her cheek to his before coming up to me. The faint smell of her perfume hits me first, filling my nose with the sweet scent of flowers, along with a note of something I've come to accept as distinctly hers.

She grips my shoulders and rises onto the tips of her toes as she repeats the same gesture with me. My parents aren't affectionate people, so it has taken me time to get used to the Martinez way of greeting family and friends with what they call a kiss on the cheek.

Now, come to think of it, I don't remember a time when Catalina has made the effort for me. She has done a remarkable job preventing any physical contact, so the opportunity has probably been avoided at all costs.

"Hi," she says as our cheeks brush, sending a current of energy rippling across my skin and down the length of my spine as my stubble rubs against the soft skin of her cheek.

The contact can't last more than two seconds, but my heart racing in my chest makes me feel like I've spent the last ten minutes on the treadmill.

Pull yourself together, I tell myself as she steps away.

I've never been the type to be nervous around women, but then again, most women actually *want* to spend time with me—whether that be purely platonic or more. Catalina, on the other hand, can't seem to escape me quickly enough, although I'm starting to realize it's a defense mechanism rather than a way to snub me. She keeps most people at a distance, and I've never tried to fight my way out of that category.

Well, until now.

Her eyes flicker over me once more before her sister tugs her toward the decorated bookshelves beside our TV. They're a recent addition to the apartment, and one Aiden insisted on us buying to add some personal touches to our drab space. He added a few model airplanes that he's collected over the years while the rest of the shelves showcase all the LEGOs I've built since college.

I wasn't really a LEGO kid growing up since my parents didn't believe in kids having fun, but once I entered adulthood, I discovered the soothing hobby, and it stuck.

Catalina reaches out for a limited edition set I built a year ago before she pulls her hand back and tucks it behind her.

"Told you Luke was a nerd like you," Gaby says loud enough for me to hear.

"I am *not* a nerd." I walk up to them.

"Exactly how much have you spent on resale LEGO sets?"

"There's a market for those?" Catalina asks with pinched brows.

"Ask Luke. If he's not working, he's online shopping." Gaby grins.

My gaze narrows. "I stopped doing that months ago."

"Why?" Catalina turns to look at me.

Aiden laughs behind me, and I flip him off without looking.

Gaby's eyes sparkle. "Yeah, Luke. Why do you avoid resellers again?"

These assholes know exactly why, but I refuse to give them the satisfaction of answering.

Catalina looks around when I don't respond. "What happened?"

"Because he was scammed." Aiden volunteers the information.

"How?" Catalina asks with a ghost of a smile on her lips.

I huff.

"It's quite the story," Aiden, my future ex-best friend, says with a smirk.

"He can tell it over dinner." Gaby walks over to the round table and takes a seat in her usual spot.

Aiden follows her lead and settles into the seat beside her. Catalina chooses to sit next to her sister, leaving me with the empty chair between her and Aiden.

Despite Aiden reassuring me that he doesn't care if I'm

interested in his ex, I can't help second-guessing his statement as I drop into my chair beside them. Not because I'm uninterested in Catalina, but rather I'm unsure if she will be willing to give me a chance. Given her history with my best friend, I wouldn't expect her to.

You're getting ahead of yourself, I remind myself.

Each of us serves ourselves a generous helping of lasagna and salad while Gaby tells the story of how I'm no longer allowed to help after almost chopping my finger off while cutting an onion.

"It was practically a paper cut," I say when Catalina cringes.

"Paper cut?" Gaby gawks. "You needed ten stitches."

"Good thing he knows a doctor," Aiden adds before shoving a forkful of salad in his mouth.

Catalina turns toward me, and her knee brushes against mine, sparks flying off my skin from the fleeting moment.

"So what's the story with getting scammed with LEGOs?" she asks.

And here I had hoped she would forget about that particular conversation.

Aiden chuckles while Gaby giggles under her breath.

I sigh as I come to terms with not getting out of this. "I was played."

"How?"

My teeth grind together at the sight of Aiden's smile.

Fuck him very much.

When I don't answer right away, Gaby does. "Someone sold him a fake set."

Catalina's eyes widen. "No."

"Yup." I clench my jaw.

"When did you realize it wasn't the real thing?"

"When the pieces said LECO on them."

She is trying her absolute hardest not to laugh. I can see it in the way her shoulders bunch up and her lips press together so tightly, they begin to turn white.

I desperately want to hear the sound, so I admit something that not even Aiden knows.

"Wanna know the worst part?"

She nods, her eyes glimmering from withheld laughter, and damn, I love being on the receiving end of her amusement.

"The guy who conned me out of a thousand dollars?" I pause for dramatic effect. "He couldn't be more than thirteen years old."

She finally cracks, and a soft laugh pours from her lips, feeding me in a way food never can. Catalina isn't the type for loud belly laughs that leave someone's stomach aching, but I've never heard a better sound than the one she makes because of *me*.

CHAPTER TWELVE
Catalina

My sister and I load up the dishwasher while Aiden and Luke hang out in the living room. At some point between helping my sister pack away the leftovers and scrubbing some burnt bits off the ceramic casserole dish, Aiden and Luke brought out the unopened Galactic Command Base LEGO set.

I sneak a few glances over my shoulder as they pull out the countless plastic bags full of pieces. The pile grows, along with the crease between Aiden's brows as he picks up the thick builder's manual. I'm tempted to grab it out of his hands, but I hold back solely because I don't want to feed into my sister and Aiden's attempt at keeping me here. It didn't take me long to realize why they were trying to hype Luke up to me, and on more than one occasion I wanted to tell them it was pointless.

I can see with my own two eyes that Luke is exactly my type, and the LEGO set is the final nail in the coffin.

Aiden flips through the manual. "I was never into these things as a kid."

"I heard you were too busy playing doctor with your sister's stuffed animals to be bothered," Luke replies.

My lips pinch together to muffle the sound of my laughter, and my sister doesn't look any better off, based on the way she presses her hand to her mouth.

Aiden and Luke keep taking jabs at each other while they organize all the plastic bags by number. They've been like this all night, making Gabriela and me laugh numerous times with the way they argue like brothers. It's funny to watch, especially since I've never hung around Luke long enough to see him be more himself.

More...*imperfect.*

It's obvious why my sister likes spending time with these two. At first, when she invited me over for dinner, I was skeptical as to why she wanted me to hang around the three of them, but now I understand that Gabriela is creating her own family with Aiden, and she would like me to be part of it, even if it means getting along with Luke.

Truth be told, it isn't that much of a hardship. Luke has a way of making anyone feel comfortable in his presence, which was something I hadn't cared to notice before because I was intent on focusing on the bad.

Easygoing? More like putting on a façade.

Polite? He must be faking niceties because our loved ones are getting married, not because he is actually a nice guy who wants to make people feel welcomed.

Friendly? No way he willingly wants to talk to me of all

people. No one else bothers with me, so why would he try so hard?

The longer I think about how I've assumed the worst about Luke, the more ashamed I feel because it's only taken a few genuine encounters to realize he really is the kind of guy who likes going out of his way to help others.

Some people really are undeniably good, and in a world like ours, we could use more of them.

"Cata!" Aiden calls from the living room.

"What?"

"Come over here."

"In a sec."

I'm about to start cleaning the sink, but my sister drags me along with her. "We can finish that later."

"What is it?" I ask as Gabriela stops in front of Aiden and Luke, who are seated on the floor beside the coffee table covered with a bunch of plastic bags full of LEGO pieces.

"We need your help," Aiden says.

"We?" Luke stares at him with an arched brow.

"*I* need your help." Aiden groans, and I bite back a laugh. He is a worse actor than my sister, and that's saying something. If I wasn't excited by the idea of helping build the LEGO set, I'd be annoyed at Aiden's obvious matchmaking attempt.

My fingers tremble with excitement, but I clench my hands to stop myself from reaching out to offer my assistance.

This is a trap.

Yet here I am, considering willingly falling into it anyway.

Aiden looks up at me. "Tell Luke about the time I built that IKEA bookshelf for Gaby."

"Which time are we talking about? Because it took you three tries to get it right, and when she asked for another one, you hired someone off the internet to build it for her."

"That's exactly what I thought." Luke plucks the instruction manual from Aiden's hands. "You're officially dismissed. I appreciate the offer to help, though."

Aiden doesn't look the least bit affronted when he asks, "For real?"

"I can't risk the structural integrity of the base."

A small laugh slips out of me, and Luke's head whips in my direction.

Aiden looks over at me too, his smile expanding. "You think this is funny?"

"Nope." I take a step back and accidentally bump into my sister.

Aiden scoffs. "My pride is being obliterated here, Cata. Show some damn respect."

"Aw." Gabriela kneels beside her fiancé and rubs his chest. "There. There. I'll buy you some MEGA BLOKS to practice with first."

"Aren't those for toddlers?" he asks.

"Fitting since you have the ego of one…" Luke throws the barb with a smile, earning another soft smile from me.

Aiden points an accusatory finger at me. "Stop encouraging him."

Luke doesn't bother shielding his bright grin like I do. "Don't get mad at her for finding me funny."

"I'm laughing *at* you. Not with you."

Luke shrugs. "So long as you're laughing, that's all that

matters to me."

My cheeks betray me in that moment, making him smile wider.

Dammit. One week ago, I found ten different reasons to dislike his smile, but now, he has me all torn up inside as I try to navigate this new gray area of our…friendship? Situationship? Relationship? The third feels too serious while the first feels like a lie when a single graze of his fingers across my skin leaves me flushed.

Bottom line is that I'm more confused than ever about whatever is going on between us, and I'm not sure how to best go about dealing with these newfound feelings.

"Are you going to stare at each other all night, or are we building this thing?" Aiden reaches for a plastic bag.

Before Luke has a chance to stop him from ripping it open, I steal it from his grasp. "Don't open that."

"Why not?"

I point at the number five. "It's the wrong one."

"Care to point me in the direction of the right one then?"

I take a seat on the carpet between him and Luke and search through the pile of bags until I find the correct one hidden at the bottom. When I hand it over to Aiden, he ignores me and drags my sister onto his lap instead.

I don't realize I'm looking over at Luke, wondering what he thinks of their excessive PDA until our eyes connect. His brown irises look darker in this light, and the stubble on his cheek appears thicker than usual, framing his lips.

I'm not sure how long I stare at his mouth, but it must be long enough for him to unleash another smile.

"See something you like?" he says.

Please kill me quickly.

I toss him the bag of LEGOs like it might catch on fire at any moment.

"Want me to open it for you?" The way he says it, his eyes glimmering from excitement, makes me want to say yes. I would like nothing more than to join him in building the LEGO set, but then I hesitate.

Isn't this what you always wanted?

I think back to all those visits to the mall, watching couples pick out sets together, then going back to my empty apartment to build one by myself. But when I imagined finding a partner who would want to have fun building LEGOs with me, I never thought Luke would be that person.

It's one night.

Yet it feels like a lot more than I'm ready for, so I do what I do best and pretend to be uninterested, rather than express the way I really feel.

Maybe you're more like your mom than you think.

Shit. The thought hits me hard, and I'm struggling with an overwhelming sense of sadness for the two of us and our issues expressing ourselves.

I'm set in my decision to steer clear of the Galactic Command Base right up until Luke rubs the back of his neck, looking more nervous than I've ever seen him before. His cheeks, which are usually pale, turn pink as he asks, "Will you help us out?"

Oh God. Is he acting this way because of *me*?

I was so focused on myself that I didn't consider how *he*

would feel by putting himself out there and asking me to help. Based on the wall behind us, it's obvious he doesn't need me, so that can only mean one thing.

He wants to spend more time with you.

It's not a surprise, especially when he was clear about his interest the other day when we were in the car together, but the way I feel about him orchestrating all this just so he could hang out with me makes me feel…

Shit.

It—no, he—makes me feel *good*, especially since I'm no longer plagued with guilt about liking Luke. It seems silly to do so after my sister and Aiden clearly went out of their way to have us spend time together.

It's not like this can go anywhere.

No, but you can still enjoy yourself while you're in town, a small voice in the back of my head challenges the louder one.

It doesn't take much for Luke to have me reconsidering my choice tonight. Maybe it's something about the way his whole face turns a bright shade of pink as he avoids direct eye contact, or perhaps it's the small but noticeable slump in his shoulders when I don't speak up right away that has me questioning everything.

The thought of turning him down makes me feel worse about the whole situation, so I grab the manual and open it to the very first page. "I'll help on one condition."

"What?"

"You promise not to build any of it without me." My nerves make my voice shake near the end, but I straighten my back and exude more confidence than I feel.

If I'm going to start this project with him, then I'm going to see it through from beginning to end, even if it means spending endless hours with Luke in the process. It's not like it would be a chore or anything, seeing as I'm starting to enjoy his company instead of avoiding it.

Luke holds out his hand, and I reach for it while pretending the tightness in my stomach is from the anticipation of building the LEGO set rather than his touch.

"You've got yourself a deal."

CHAPTER THIRTEEN

Luke

aking a deal with Catalina to not build the set without her is a no-brainer. Since I bought the Galactic Command Base because of her, of course I'd rather spend the time building it together, but I'm not about to admit that.

Together, we spend the next thirty minutes sipping *coquito* and working while Gaby and Aiden hang out with us. Eventually, the couple disappears into his room, leaving me alone with Catalina. I expect her to get skittish once she's alone with me, but she seems to not care about their absence and carries on with building.

We spend the next hour passing pieces back and forth, and I repeatedly ask her for the manual despite not really needing it, strictly because I enjoy the graze of her fingers against my skin far too much. A man like me could get addicted to a touch like hers. That much has become clear after tonight,

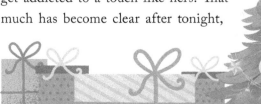

along with my inability to stop myself from every opportunity to touch her.

Eventually, our movements start to lag, and I reluctantly call it a night once I catch Catalina stifling her yawn.

"Do you need me to take you home?" I ask when she stands and stretches her legs.

She cringes. "Gabriela offered, but…" Her gaze swings to Aiden's shut door. No obvious sounds come from the room, so most likely they both just fell asleep.

"I don't mind driving you."

Her brows knit together. "Um, that's all right. I can call for a ride. There's no need to go out of your way to take me home."

"It's the least I can do after you saved Aiden earlier from making a huge mistake."

Her cheeks turn a light pink. "It's fine, really. I can just call for someone on the app and save you the trouble."

Rather than push her on the subject, I motion toward her phone. "If you insist." I sit back against the couch and bite back a smile.

Her eyes narrow at my mouth. "Thank you, though. That's…sweet of you." She trips over the words.

"Do you want me to get you another drink while you wait?"

"A drink?" Her brows pinch together. "The car will be here in… *Forty minutes*?" The pitch of her voice rises. "Seriously? And since when are rides this expensive?"

"Since all the rich people started moving here." I swallow the last swig of *coquito* before placing the cup on the coffee table.

"This is ridiculous." Catalina pockets her phone with a

scowl.

"My offer still stands."

She takes a deep breath. "All right. Thanks."

With a grin, I head to the front door and pluck my keys off the hook while Catalina cancels her ride and grabs her purse. When she turns to the door, I'm already holding her coat out. I expect her to take it from me, but she pleasantly surprises me by turning around and inserting her arms into both holes instead.

My fingers graze her neck as I pull her hair free from underneath the coat, earning a sharp inhale from her that makes my smile widen.

She might *pretend* to be unaffected by my presence, but her reactions tell a different story. One with an alternative ending where she doesn't resist me at every single turn, but rather accepts that there is something...special between us. Something worth exploring, even if it scares her.

She spins on her heel to face me. Something pulls me toward her, and before she knows what I'm doing, I reach down and help button her coat.

She stands there, still as a statue, while I make my way down the row of buttons, taking my sweet time while her chest rises with each ragged breath.

"All good?"

"Yup."

"You sure?"

"Yes." Catalina doesn't look me in the eyes until I open the door and motion for her to exit before me.

"Thank you," she says in a soft voice that can hardly be

heard over the sound of me zipping my jacket.

"You're welcome." I lock the door behind us and lead her to my SUV. It's a used model I purchased last year after my crappy car gave out on me, and one I'm grateful for given Michigan's winter weather. My last one didn't have blind spot sensors or seat warmers, so I appreciate the upgrades.

When I get in the car, I immediately turn on the seat warmers for both of us and arrange our heater settings, making sure Catalina's vents are open and facing her.

She looks at me with a curious expression that has me asking, "What?"

"My dad always does that for my mom," she says it with a hint of apprehension, as if the confession might cost her something.

I've seen Aiden and his dad do the same thing countless times for the women sitting beside them, so I never thought much of it until Catalina mentioned it.

She yawns as I pull out of the parking spot. My car might have a back-up camera, but that doesn't stop me from placing my hand on the back of Catalina's head rest and turning to look back. My fingers graze the nape of her neck in the process, earning a slight inhale from her and a little zap of electricity along the tips of my fingers.

Teasing Catalina might be my favorite kind of punishment yet, knowing I'm only tempting myself in the process.

The drive to her parents' house isn't a long one, so I decide to make the most of it since she has been in such a giving mood tonight.

"Have you made any progress on your maid of honor

speech?"

She turns in her seat, stealing my attention away from the road for a second before I get a grip on myself and the steering wheel.

"Why are you asking?"

"Because I'm curious how long you plan on putting it off."

She stares at me for a few blinks before speaking. "I'm not usually a procrastinator, but…" Her voice drifts off.

"What?"

"I'm not exactly good at sharing my feelings."

"Really? I would've never noticed."

She smacks my arm with a soft laugh.

"It's not easy," I say. "Took me far too long to write my best man speech if we're being honest."

"Ugh. At least you're done! The idea of pouring my heart out…of trying to make people *laugh*?" she says the last word with an endearing crinkling of her nose. "Safe to say I suck at that, so yeah, I've been putting it off for as long as humanly possible."

"You know, I'm not one to brag—"

She scoffs.

I grin. "But I'm pretty good at both of those things."

"Of course you are," she mutters under her breath.

"What's that supposed to mean?"

"You're good at *everything*."

"No. Definitely not everything, but I'm flattered you think so highly of me." My comment earns me a soft slap to the shoulder, followed by a tinkle of laughter from the woman beside me.

Joking about my perfectionism has become a defense mechanism because I'd rather make light of a subject that causes me discomfort than give people too much insight into why I act that way in the first place.

No one is perfect, but I spent far too long agonizing over being the best in every single way to please my parents, only to realize a little too late that I was hurting myself in the process. It took me a while to accept that messing up is a normal part of life, and I'm now a recovering perfectionist.

Catalina sighs. "Well, my mom couldn't stop raving about your speech, so I know it's good."

"I could help you." The words leave my mouth in a rush. "If you want me to, that is."

"You'd help me?"

"Sure."

"Why?"

I raise a brow. "Because you're running out of time."

"I still have two weeks."

"And how have the last sixty-three weeks been going since you found out you'd be the maid of honor?"

She makes a sour face.

"I thought as much," I say.

"No need to gloat."

"But it's so cute to see you get all flustered when I do."

She bares her teeth at me.

"Don't tell me you're too proud to accept any help."

"I'm not proud. I'm...nervous." She bites down on her bottom lip.

"About?"

"I don't want you to judge me."

I shake my head. "I won't."

"You say that *now*."

"And I'll say it every day until I've convinced you to let me help."

"But *I'm* the one who is supposed to be writing the speech. Not you."

"Maybe you just need someone to bounce ideas off?" I ask.

She stares at me. "And you're that person?"

"Seeing as I wrote a speech worthy of your mother's raving, I think so."

"What do you want in exchange?"

"Who says I want something?"

"*Everyone* wants something. You're no exception, Captain America."

My upper lip curls. "I'm growing to resent that nickname."

She tries to hide her smile, but I catch it in the window's reflection.

"So, what do you want?" she asks after a few moments.

"I'm not sure you're ready for an honest answer." My response seems to pique her interest.

"Shouldn't I be the one to decide that?"

My heart picks up speed. "Truth is, I just want to spend more time with you."

"Why?" Her lips curl into a small frown.

"What do you mean *why*?"

"I don't understand."

"Then allow me to make myself clear one last time," I say as I pull the car to a halt in front of a red light. "I'm interested in you, which means I want to spend time getting to know you."

She tugs at a loose button on her coat. "There's not much to know."

"You do a good job making people think that, but I know what you're doing."

She bites down on the inside of her cheek. "I'm only here for two more weeks."

"So I've been told."

"This can't go anywhere." Her pointer finger swings between us.

"Why not?"

"Because I'm leaving after the wedding."

That might be true, but that doesn't mean we can't make the most of the time she is here.

"Fine," I answer, making her brows scrunch together.

Does she really expect me to give up so easily? If so, now I'm equal parts insulted and motivated to prove her wrong.

"Making the most of two weeks with you seems better than spending a lifetime wondering what could've been."

She groans under her breath. "Someone has been watching one too many episodes of *The Duke Who Seduced Me* with Gabriela."

"Well, she *did* tell me to take notes."

Catalina shakes her head with a smile, and I'm so distracted by the sight that I miss the light turning green until she pokes me in the arm.

"Go."

I press my foot against the accelerator. She mulls over my

offer in silence, and I decide to keep quiet so she can come to a decision of her own.

It takes her a few minutes, but she turns to face me. "*If* I agree to let you help me..."

I smile.

She glares. "I said if!"

"Mm. Carry on."

She throws her arms up. "Ugh. I'm regretting this already."

"Regretting *what*?" I tease.

"Agreeing to let you help me."

"Is that a request?"

She makes another noise of discontent, and I release a short laugh and say, "I'd love nothing more than to help you."

"You're annoyingly smug right now."

"And you're adorably flustered."

She dips her head in a poor attempt to hide her burning cheeks.

I decide to put her out of her misery by saying, "You won't regret this. I promise."

I may have won this battle, but the war against Catalina's walls has only begun, and I'm looking forward to the process of tearing each one down.

shake it before
you taste it

CHAPTER FOURTEEN

Catalina

Earlier tonight, Luke sent me a text, inviting me to come check out the new espresso machine he installed in the first-floor break room during his last shift.

I feel like an eager child as I count the minutes until my thirty-minute break, and I have to tell myself more than once to calm down and rein in my excitement.

It's just coffee, I silently groan when I catch myself glancing at the clock for the third time in ten minutes.

At three a.m., I head down to the first floor with a lightness in my chest that I haven't felt all night, and it's because of Luke. Tonight's shift has been hard. It isn't as bad as the time Luke caught me crying, but it has still sucked, especially when I had to talk to Sarah's parents about her arrangements.

I shelve the thought and focus on happy ones instead...or as happy as I can feel knowing Luke plans on getting started on my maid of honor speech straight away. My feet should be dragging at the idea, but I find myself speed-walking to the break room so I don't waste any more time.

I enter the small room to find Luke already at the espresso machine, scrolling on his phone while waiting for a ceramic mug to finish filling up, although I'm quickly distracted by the decorations scattered around the room.

What the break room lacks in space it makes up for in holiday decor. Every empty table has a miniature poinsettia placed at the center, and paper snowflakes hang from the ceiling. Gifts for the town's toy drive are piled high in one corner while a corkboard has stringed lights tacked above a list of events coming up throughout December.

"They did a nice job with the place, right?"

"Yeah," I say, turning my head to find him already staring at me.

Luke has this effect on me that should be alarming. The way my heartbeat escalates from a single smile—from a damn glimmer in his eyes as his gaze travels over me—is exactly what I would want…while being everything I shouldn't pursue.

Regardless of how Luke makes me feel, it doesn't change the fact that I'm leaving at the start of new year for my next job while he will stay here, building a life and career for himself.

You're just having fun together. That's all, I tell myself as he pockets his phone and gives me his full, undivided attention.

It's starting to feel less like fun and more like—well, more.

I lose my train of thought as his dark eyes rake over me, tracing an invisible path from my face to the hem of my scrub pants.

"Reindeer." His flirtatious smile makes my insides clench. "Huh?"

He tips his chin in my direction. "Today's scrubs."

I stare down at my clothes like I'm seeing them for the first time. "Oh. Right. Reindeer."

"You've got quite the collection going for yourself."

My cheeks flush. "Meaning?"

"I haven't seen you repeat a single scrub set yet."

I press my lips together to stop myself from asking why he's been keeping track.

"How many scrubs do you have?" he asks when I don't say anything.

"That's a personal question." A hint of defensiveness bleeds into my voice.

"I'll trade you a cup of coffee for an answer then." He grabs the full mug from the machine and holds it out for me.

I blink at it. "You made me a cup?"

"Technically, all I did was pop the hazelnut pod inside the machine and let it do the rest, but sure. I made it just for you."

I try to look past the fact that he really did buy my favorite flavor pods—and fail miserably. Damn him for being sweet and thoughtful. Damn him straight to hell because if he keeps this up, I'll never survive the next two weeks without catching some kind of feelings.

My heart squeezes at his gesture. "Thank you."

He acknowledges my comment with a dip of his head. "If you don't tell me how many scrubs you really have, I'll assume it's over three hundred."

I gawk. "That's ridiculous!"

"Four hundred?"

"*No.*"

"Then how many?"

We stare at each other for a few seconds without blinking before I let out a resigned sigh. "Ballpark number? Probably sixty. Or maybe seventy—" His lips twitch. "I stopped counting after fifty, so technically I don't know."

He laughs to himself. "That's not as bad as I thought."

I make grabby hands for the cup of coffee, and he passes it to me. His fingers brush across the inside of my wrist, and I bite back a smile as familiar butterflies unleash in my belly.

I'm catching on to Luke's slick ways of initiating contact, but I pretend to be oblivious because I secretly like him touching me. It makes me feel desired, and I'll be damned if I ruin it by pretending that I don't like it.

Luke tips his head toward the empty table in one corner of the break room. We walk over to it, and he pulls out my seat and waits for me to sit before taking the one across from me.

We will not swoon. We will not—

He interrupts my inner mantra with another question. "How do you travel with all of them?"

"I bring an extra suitcase packed with all my scrubs. Since I come home to my parents' house twice a year, I switch out the old ones with the others."

"Smart. So you have different ones for seasons and holidays?"

"Yup. I made a bet with Gabriela last year, though, so I'm only allowed to treat myself to a new one every season."

"So four a year?"

"Yes."

"Why would you do that?"

"Because we both have addictions we're trying to overcome." It's not *my* fault that my favorite medical clothing company drops new apparel every few months, right? I'm clearly a victim of consumer culture and capitalism.

He leans forward with a smile, turning my insides to mush. "This sounds serious."

"Tell me about it. If I break my scrub-buying-ban, then I'm screwed."

"How so?"

"That's between me and her."

He stares at me thoughtfully. "Based on your facial expression, I assume it's bad."

"Your assumption isn't wrong."

"Have you considered seeking medical attention for this so-called addiction?"

I fight a smile. "No."

"Good thing you know a couple of doctors then. I'd be more than happy to help."

I motion between us. "Wouldn't this be a conflict of interest?"

"Depends on if you want there to be one." His eyes sparkle like a thousand gems are trapped beneath the surface.

Desire coils in my stomach, my muscles clenching as I take a deep breath. "Let's get through the wedding first—my addiction can wait."

His smirk slips. "Speaking of weddings, did you bring a notebook?"

"Yeah." I pull a small one out of my front pocket and toss it on the table.

He reaches for it and flips to a blank page. "We should start with the basics."

"Like?"

"What's your favorite memory of Gabriela and you?"

"That's the basics?"

"Seems like as good a place as any to start."

"I—" I guess in theory that's a smart idea, so rather than push back on his request, I think of my answer.

I rifle through my memory bank while sipping my coffee. "Well…we used to dress up like a bride and groom and play house together."

He leans back in his chair and crosses his arms, drawing my attention toward the muscles straining against the fabric of his scrubs.

"Who was the bride?" he asks for a second time when I don't answer the first.

"Most of the time it was both of us."

"And the other times?"

My eyes roll. "Gabriela would beg me to play the groom."

"And I'm guessing you couldn't say no."

"Are you kidding? She would break down crying any time I suggested we switch roles."

He chuckles under his breath.

"Gabriela and I would invite our parents and stuffed animals to all of our fake weddings. We'd bring out our tea set and have a reception before moving into the karaoke portion of the event. God, we spent hours singing and dancing on the tops of our dad's feet. My dad always had a special song for both of us, and I'm not sure how he didn't go crazy listening to the same two over and over again."

When I look up, I find Luke's gaze pinned to my face and a small quirk to his lips.

"What?"

"Nothing. It's a good story…"

"But?"

"But nothing." He glances away.

My mouth falls open. "Luke Darling. Are you lying to me right now?"

"No." His cheeks turn pink.

"Oh my God." The idea of Luke being terrible at something like lying makes me laugh. "I'm not sure if anyone has told you this, but you might be the worst liar to exist."

He grumbles something incoherent under his breath.

"It's cute," I say.

My comment seems to gain his attention as he asks, "What is?"

"The fact that you can't lie to save your life."

"Shut up." He scrubs a hand down his face as if that can wipe the pink flush from his cheeks.

"Aw. Look at you getting all shy on me."

"You know what? You can figure out the speech yourself." He tosses the notebook on the table and moves to stand.

I grab his arm to stop him from leaving. "No! You promised to help me."

His eyes narrow. "I didn't anticipate such a hostile working environment."

"Hostile?"

"Yes, because you, Catalina Martinez, are a bully."

My hand tightens around his wrist. "Excuse me?"

"You heard me."

Don't you dare laugh.

His eyes flicker with awareness, as if he can read my mind. "I'm going to add all this to my HR complaint."

"This report seems to be getting longer by the day."

"At this rate, I'll be able to write a tell-all book about you."

I roll my eyes. "I'm not that interesting."

He stuns me momentarily with a dazzling smile. "That's where you're wrong."

I suck in a breath.

"Everything about you interests me." His gaze flickers over my face, and I find my own cheeks warming under his perusal.

His lips part, but whatever he is about to say gets cut off by a male nurse entering the room.

"Doctor Darling! I had hoped to find you here. Eileen has been looking all over for you. The patient in 2B who had a gastric suction needs your help."

"What's the status on the patient?" Luke jumps into doctor mode as he reaches for his stethoscope on the table and places it around his neck, and I'll be the first to admit his quick transition from charming flirt to authoritative medical professional is hot.

He might not wear a white coat, but the energy he exudes screams that he is the man in charge.

The nurse shakes his head. "Oh. They're fine, but you missed a signature on a patient's discharge form."

The muscles in Luke's shoulders relax. "Why wasn't I

paged?"

"Eileen wanted to, but I thought I could buy you some more time for your break."

"Thanks." Luke sighs. "I'll be right there."

The nurse says goodbye before leaving.

Luke rubs the back of his neck. "I should go. Eileen is probably losing her mind over incomplete paperwork."

"Best of luck to you."

His lips quirk at the corners. "Let's pick back up on the speech tomorrow?"

"I'm not working."

"I know." His smirk turns into a full-blown smile.

Meeting up somewhere outside of work without Gabriela or Aiden feels serious in a way. Like Luke and I are making a conscious effort to spend time together without our friends or my family serving as a buffer.

He just wants to help you.

Yeah, all while simultaneously trying to get closer to me in any way he can.

He rubs the back of his neck again—a nervous tic I'm starting to easily recognize, and one I'm beginning to enjoy drawing out of him. Even the pink flush in his cheeks returns with a vengeance, although this time from nervousness rather than being caught in a little white lie.

Damn him for making me think his self-consciousness is endearing. I, of all people, should be turned off by the idea of someone being vulnerable, but Luke going from confident and flirtatious to nervous and uncertain draws me in, especially when compared to how confident he was only a few moments ago with the nurse.

"Where are you thinking?" I ask.

"We could meet at Nightcap?"

"The new bar in the Historic District?" It's heavily inspired by the roaring twenties and speakeasies, with cocktails they serve in tiny bathtubs and a hidden door in the back leading to a secret bar and menu, and I've wanted to go there ever since they opened a few months ago.

"Yeah. You mentioned something about it at dinner the other night."

My brows rise. All I remember saying was that Gabriela betrayed me by going to the grand opening while I was out of town, so the fact that he is offering to take me makes my head swim with possibilities I can no longer ignore.

If I had a sense of self-preservation, I would come up with a reason to say no. This *thing* between us can't go anywhere, but Luke seems intent on trying anyway, so if he ends up getting hurt once I have to leave, that's on him.

Him? What about you?

There is no way I will get attached to someone in two short weeks. I've always been cautious to a fault, and I'm not about to lose myself in some whirlwind romance better suited for a holiday made-for-TV movie than real life.

The thought alone makes me want to snort.

"So?" His question hangs in the air.

"You know what? Sure. I've been wanting to go there, and this speech isn't going to write itself."

"Perfect. It's a date." He winks before turning to leave.

I don't correct him on the fact that it isn't a date.

I don't remind him that we are working on a speech, not spending time getting to know each other.

I don't do anything but smile and wave as he exits the break room, taking the smallest, thinnest sliver of my heart along with him.

CHAPTER FIFTEEN

Luke

'**ve** been on plenty of dates, but I don't remember any of them making me this nervous. At least not since my very first one.

For the third time in ten minutes, I check my text thread with Catalina, making sure I told her the right time to meet up at Nightcap. I had offered to pick her up, but she was determined to order a ride through an app, so I dropped the idea. Part of me wanted to insist, but I let her be, knowing that pushing her on the subject might make her uncomfortable.

Catalina doesn't seem like the type to respond well to an overbearing alpha type, and luckily, I don't fall into that category. I'm not sure if that makes me a progressive male or a stupid one because she is already twenty minutes late—and counting.

Maybe she decided to ditch your sorry ass.

I wouldn't blame her, seeing as I'm the one who labeled us meeting up

outside of work "a date" in the first place. If she backed out of our plan while claiming food poisoning or something else, I'd be disappointed but not surprised.

I battle between calling her or casually texting to ask where she is, but before I can decide which option seems less desperate, the front door swings open. A heavy gust of wind pummels into the people standing nearest to the bar's entryway, parting the crowd that formed there. A red-faced Catalina is easy to spot with her off-white peacoat, jeans, and a knitted hat with two pompoms attached to the top.

She looks around before her gaze lands on me, and the rosiness in her cheeks intensifies as our eyes lock. My heart rate picks up, the beats gaining speed as she walks over to the booth I saved.

I slide across the leather seat and stand to greet her.

"Hey." She rubs at her arms aggressively. "I'm sorry I'm late." She pauses after every word due to her teeth clattering together.

I'm not sure what possesses me to wrap my arms around her and pull her against me, but one moment she is looking up at me with her head tilted back, and the next she is sinking against my body with a sigh.

"Did you walk here or something?" I joke.

"Yes." She digs her face into my sweater. "Two different rides cancelled on me, so I braved the weather instead."

I'm not able to enjoy the feel of her because my anger takes hold. "What the hell."

I pull away, but she lets out a growly protest and tugs me back with a "not yet."

I hope she can't hear the way my heart furiously pounds at her proximity, or actually, maybe I do. That way, she can be well aware of how much her closeness affects me.

I'm not the type to hide my feelings behind mixed signals and a game of chase. If I like a woman, I make it obvious where I stand, and with Catalina, I'm about as subtle as a flashing neon sign at midnight.

"You should've called me to come pick you up," I say, fighting the urge to shake her.

"I thought the walk would be good for me."

"Good for what? Pneumonia?"

She muffles her laugh with my sweater, easing my irritation slightly.

I pull her into my side of the booth and wrap my arm around her, tucking her body closer to mine until there is no gap between us. Catalina fits perfectly, like a missing puzzle piece clicking into place, and I wonder how I've spent the last two years avoiding her.

Because you didn't know what you were missing.

Now that I do, I plan on taking advantage of every single opportunity.

"You're lucky if you don't get sick," I say once she stops shuddering beside me.

"I rarely do." She sniffles.

"I'd be shocked if you didn't. It's what? Zero degrees out?"

She looks up at me with watering eyes. "Gabriela will kill me if I get sick before her wedding. Plus, my mom is planning a *parranda*—"

"A what?"

"*Una parranda.* It's like Christmas caroling, but we go to people's houses and have a party at the end." She smiles, and all the noise in the bar and the worry I have about her getting sick fade away as I soak in the look of pure happiness on her face.

"Can I join?" I ask without hesitation. If a *parranda* makes Catalina look like that, I want to be a part of it, solely because she clearly cares about it.

She bites down on her bottom lip. "Aren't you working on Saturday?"

"Did you memorize my schedule?"

"No." Her cheeks deepen in color.

"It's okay if you did. I'll think it's cute, in a stalkerish kind of way."

She exhales loudly. "Aiden might've mentioned it."

"And you remembered? I'm flattered by your attention to detail."

She rolls her eyes. "Are you always this exasperating?"

"Depends on if I'm in the presence of a beautiful woman like you or not."

She looks down while tucking a strand of hair behind her ear.

"So…this Saturday?" I ask.

"Aren't you working?"

"I can get my shift covered."

"All right. If you insist—"

"I do."

She fights a smile and loses. "I'll text you the info once my mom sends it to me."

"Sounds like a plan."

Her face contorts before she sneezes, the high-pitched sound making me laugh.

"Ugh." She drops her head back against the booth. "If I get sick…"

"I *did* offer to pick you up." *Way to rub it in, Luke.*

"I was being stubborn, but I learned my lesson the hard way." She sinks deeper into my side with a sigh.

Giving her any more grief about her decision to decline my ride feels pointless, since the end result led to her pressed against me, so I decide to let it go with one last request.

"Next time, save yourself the pneumonia and call me."

She tilts her head back and smirks. "Who said there'll be a next time?"

"Oh. I have no doubt in my mind."

Her eyes narrow. "Confident much?"

"With you? Never."

A server comes over, and we both order drinks.

"Have you worked on your speech at all since yesterday?" I ask.

"No."

Perfect. I had hoped as much since I want to stall the speech-writing process for as long as humanly possible until she calls me out on it.

Catalina's hands shake as she pulls the notebook from the inner pocket of her coat. I pluck it from her grasp, drop it on the table, and trap her hands between mine to warm them up faster.

"Now you're just finding reasons to keep touching me."

The soft, contented sigh she lets out goes to my head and

other places that have no business being turned on right now.

"Am I that obvious?"

"I don't think you have a single subtle bone in your body."

"I'm not sure whether or not to take that as an insult."

Her lips quirk at the corners. "Let's leave it open to interpretation then."

It takes a few minutes to warm up her hands, and by then, our conversation turns back to the speech.

I reluctantly let her go so she can freely open the notebook.

"Are you in the mood for a sappy speech or a funny one?" I ask.

"How's yours?"

"A mix of both."

"Wait. You can be funny?" she asks it with a straight face.

I glare before she breaks out into laughter.

Damn. I've never been so affected by the sound of someone else's happiness before, nor have I craved finding other ways to elicit the same response again.

She nudges me with her shoulder. "I'm kidding. I think I want a mix too. Too much emotion from me might make people uncomfortable."

"Why?"

"Most of them think I don't have any." The casual way she talks about herself pierces through my chest.

"What makes you think that?"

She stares at her notebook like the page is full of notes rather than blank lines.

"Catalina?"

Her deep sigh feels like I'm hit dead center in the chest

with a heavy weight. "I know what some people say about me behind my back."

I've never wanted to punch something—or *someone* for that matter—more.

She raises her fist and lifts her thumb. "Quiet. Bitter." She holds up another finger. "Cold and stuck-up." Her middle and ring fingers both rise. "The not-so-nice Martinez sister." She wiggles her pinkie finger.

I grab her hand and interlock our fingers. "Enough of that."

"What?" Her brows tug together. "You know it's true."

I shake my head. "What I know is that opinions are just that. *Opinions*, not facts. And frankly, anyone who thinks that about you sure as hell doesn't deserve to have you prove them wrong."

Catalina might keep her distance from others, but that doesn't make her emotionless or bitter, and I hate myself for ever giving anyone's incorrect assumption about her a single ounce of attention. Sure, a very small group of people around town have described her as withdrawn and disinterested in making connections with others, which usually doesn't fare well in a small community, but I'm starting to realize Catalina *likes* people, she just doesn't want to.

"Are they though? It's not like I make an effort to have a ton of friends."

"Why not?"

She takes so long to answer, I expect her not to, but then she surprises me when she says, "I've always been shier than Gabriela. More self-conscious and less likely to put myself out there, so people make their own assumptions about me."

Tension builds at the base of my neck. "You know what they say about people who assume?"

Her cutting laugh makes me frown. "Yeah, well, I don't try to prove them wrong either."

"If they made an effort to get to know you—a real effort— they'd think differently."

Her smile is sad. "Some people do try, but I'm not the easiest person to talk to. I'm not exactly…likable."

"Bullshit." My arm tightens around her until I can't tell where my body ends and hers begins. "Being slow to warm up to people doesn't make you unlikable. At least not to me."

It's obvious that Catalina isn't stuck-up or rude like some people might assume based off one interaction, but rather, she is a shy, cautious person who dislikes the unknown.

She looks down at her lap again. "I guess."

"I *know*. And for what it's worth, I'm glad you've given me a chance."

A small smile tugs at the edges of her mouth. "Really?"

"Don't let it go to your head."

"And compete against you for the town's biggest ego? I'll pass."

I glare, earning the best, softest laugh from Catalina in the process.

Over the next two hours, I collect similar sounds of contentment while we work on her speech. We both have a couple of drinks and swap stories about the happy couple until Catalina presses a hand against her stomach, claiming it hurts from laughing too much.

I tell her there is no such thing, and I plan on making her

laugh loud and often for as long as I can before she needs to leave town for her next job.

If she chooses to go.

I haven't considered an alternative option to Catalina wanting to stay. It might be a long shot, but maybe—just maybe—she would consider sticking around for a little while longer if she had a good reason to?

Like what? You?

The idea sounds ridiculous in my own head, but then again, I'm already looking forward to the next time I get to see her, and I haven't even said good night yet, so is it really that outlandish of a thought?

Only if you don't mind getting hurt in the process.

I shelve the negativity. Spending time with Catalina feels like the most natural thing in the world, and I don't want to say goodbye at the end of the night. There is something about her that always keeps me coming back for more.

More time. More laughter. More *her.*

Thankfully, we only made it through the first paragraph of her speech, so it looks like we will have to meet up tomorrow sometime during our shifts to continue working on it.

Convenient to say the least.

Driving Catalina home was a given after she nearly froze to death during her walk over to Nightcap. After spending the last couple of hours together, sharing stories about work, our friends, and the soon-to-be married couple, I'm reluctant to call it a night.

Catalina doesn't comment on me taking the long way back to her parents' house. Instead, I play a new album from an unknown artist we both bonded over, and we sing along to the song during the drive, with her hitting the pause button every few lines so we could analyze the lyrics together.

After one date, I feel more connected to Catalina than ever, and I'm already looking forward to our next one now that our night is coming to an end. I pull into her driveway, and our little bubble pops.

I ask her to wait while I head over to open her passenger door. The cold wind hits my face, but I hardly notice it as she slides out of my SUV with a smile.

"It gets colder every year."

"You're just not used to it anymore." I shut the door behind her.

She turns to her parents' house. I place my hand on the small of her back and follow her toward the front door, where she stops and fishes for the keys inside her purse.

My heart pounds against my chest, the beats rapid and out of sync as I wait.

"So." I let the word hang as I rub the back of my neck.

Her eyes light up as she tracks the move. "What?"

"I know we talked about tomorrow, but…"

She is silent as the night surrounding us.

I continue, "I was wondering if…" I clearly can't finish a sentence to save my life.

"Yes?" Her lips pull into a knowing smirk.

There is no way she is going to make this easy on me, so I decide to get it over with.

"Would you like to hang out? Outside of working on the speech again?"

She smirks. "As friends?"

I want to kiss the cute-as-hell look off her face, and I want to do it right now. We did not spend the last two hours together, flirting over drinks and stories of our lives, for me to be put in the friend zone.

Fuck that.

Catalina sucks in a sharp breath as I wrap my hand around the back of her neck and pull her against my chest. Her eyes drop to my mouth, and I take that as an invitation to do something I've been thinking about all night, since the moment she circled her arms around me under the guise of craving body heat.

I tilt my head and lean down, not closing my eyes until I see her do so first. Her soft lips part ever so slightly right before I press my mouth against hers for the first time. A sigh slips out of her as she pulls on the front of my coat and drags me closer, eliminating any space between our bodies.

The kiss is soft but electric, making my skin tingle with anticipation as she matches my enthusiasm with her own. My other arm swoops around her, securing her against my chest as she deepens the kiss, flooding my mouth with the taste of *her*.

After a few moments, I wrench myself away, my breaths heavy and my cock thickening with desire. "Does that answer your question?"

"Mm. I might need some further clarification." She stands on the tips of her toes and seals her mouth over mine.

My head turns fuzzy with every second that passes, and

I'm not sure how much time elapses, but I don't care because the heat in my veins keeps me warm against the chill.

I thread my fingers through Catalina's hair as her arms circle around the back of my neck, holding me close while we continue kissing.

I'm unaware of how long we stand in the cold, but it doesn't matter. Heat floods my body, scorching a path from my chest directly toward my lower half that aches for her.

This is only a kiss, I try to remind myself.

Then why does it feel like so much more? a small voice in the back of my head speaks up.

The worst thing I can do to myself is get my hopes up over a woman who has no intention of sticking around, but then again, avoiding her doesn't feel like an option anymore, especially when she makes me feel like this from a single kiss.

Even if it means I get hurt in the process.

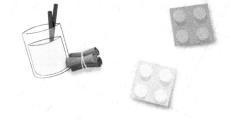

shake it before
you taste it

CHAPTER SIXTEEN
Catalina

uke Darling is kissing me like I've never been kissed before, and I'm not sure what to do with this discovery. It is better than I ever could've imagined, and my brain feels like it floated away from my body, leaving me to make some very questionable decisions tonight.

I shut my mind off and deepen the kiss. The urge to explore his body with the tips of my cold fingers becomes undeniable, and I slip my hands inside his coat and memorize the curves and planes of muscle.

His hips jut forward when I flick my tongue over his before sucking on his bottom lip. The obvious sign of his arousal makes my head spin, and my ego explodes as he shows me just how much my touch affects him.

I feel drunk off his pheromones, and for a brief moment, I wish to never sober up.

Or at least I *did* until a neighbor driving by my parents' house rudely

yells out, "Get inside before you catch a cold!"

Our lust-filled haze dies, and reality comes roaring back as I stare up at Luke with a blend of horror and fascination.

He didn't just kiss me. He ruined every kiss of my past, present, and future, reshaping my expectations and creating a craving that only he can satisfy.

It terrifies me, and I take a step back, as if adding space will somehow clear my head of all the thoughts surrounding him. He doesn't seem to share my feelings of apprehension as he steps forward and clasps my chin.

He brushes the pad of his thumb across my bottom lip. "That was…" He is breathless and his eyes are hooded as they drop to my mouth again.

I shiver, and he shakes his head. "Fuck."

I take another step back despite the desire to close the gap between us again.

"Catalina," he rasps, and my lower half pulses at the sound of pure need in his voice.

"Yes?" I keep my voice emotionless.

"Go on another date with me?"

I'm not sure what I was expecting him to say, but that was not it.

"Who said this one was a date?"

He makes a face.

"You know, for someone who looks like a dark-haired Captain America, you sure lack finesse."

"What can I say? You bring out a self-conscious side of me."

"Really?" I thought as much but hearing him confess it

aloud makes me *giddy*.

There he goes, rubbing the back of his neck again. Now that I come to think of it, he only ever does that with me, and the thought makes my chest all warm and tingly again.

Hm. Maybe I like throwing him off his game and ruining that image of confidence he puts on for everyone else.

"Are you thinking about it or…?" He doesn't finish his sentence, another habit that I suspect only happens when I'm in his proximity.

I could reject him. It would be easy to throw up some walls, protect myself from the inevitable hurt I'm bound to feel once I leave town and avoid the possible drama that could unfold if things became more serious, but at the same time, it feels like one of the most difficult decisions I've had to make in a while.

Truth is, I want to spend more time with Luke. Even if nothing serious comes out of us hanging out together, I can't deny the impulse I have to see this through, regardless of all the reasons I shouldn't.

"What do you have in mind?" I ask.

His smile comes back in full force. "Ordering takeout and working on the Galactic Command Base together at my place?"

I cross my arms and quirk a brow. "Is that Luke code for sex?"

"Shit." His cheeks, which were red from the cold, deepen in color. He tucks his hands into the front pockets of his jacket, as if to stop himself from rubbing his neck again. "Would you rather us go somewhere else? I just thought you would like to build the set with me—" he rambles before I cut him off and give his shoulder a little shove.

"I was just teasing you. That sounds perfect."

"Really?"

"Yeah. I'd rather do that than go to a restaurant or something." I've dated a few men throughout my life, and none of them have been interested in spending a night together doing something so simple yet so *me*, and I'm not about to squander the opportunity.

"So, Friday? Let's say seven p.m.?" His confidence grows, and my smile along with it.

"Sure."

"And tomorrow we'll meet up in the break room to work on the speech?"

"Only if you promise to have a cup of coffee ready for me."

"Deal." He drops a quick kiss on my lips, and they tingle as he steps away from me.

I turn and unlock the front door, keeping my excitement hidden as I quietly slip inside the house. The last thing I want to do is wake my parents up and have them question who I was staying out until midnight with.

The door clicks shut behind me, and I press my back against it. With a trembling hand, I brush the pads of my fingers over my swollen lips.

If one kiss has me feeling this light-headed, I have no idea what the future will bring me, but I do know one thing. Whatever happens between Luke Darling and me might be temporary, but this connection is anything but fleeting, and it absolutely scares me.

Thankfully, I don't get sick with pneumonia or the flu after my dumb decision to walk to the bar last night, but unfortunately, I'm suffering from a different kind of illness.

Early signs of lovesickness.

Or at least that's what my best friends keep saying in the Work Wives group chat after I catch them up on yesterday's date.

NANCY
If you DIDN'T like him, I'd be concerned.

NANCY
I mean look at him.

She attaches a photo from Luke's social media profile where he's dressed up like an elf while he and an older volunteer, who is wearing a Santa costume, were photographed delivering gifts to children at the hospital.

MONICA
You know how many men can look that good in a ridiculous getup like that?

WINNY
Forget Luke. What about the silver fox dressed up like Santa?

NANCY
...

MONICA
I can't tell if you're joking.

MONICA

Please tell me you are.

ME

I sure hope so.

WINNY

What? He's hot.

MONICA

Yeah, in a "will ask for a senior discount at restaurants and movie theaters" kind of way.

Winny sends an eye-rolling emoji.

ME

Can we focus on the subject at hand?

MONICA

Is Catalina willingly asking us to talk about her feelings? Someone call Doctor Darling because I think I'm having a heart attack.

NANCY

Seriously I'm never getting over his name. *swoons*

NANCY

Can you imagine being called Nurse Darling?

ME

No, seeing as I'm not thinking about marriage after ONE date.

NANCY

Does that mean there are more in your future?

ME

Maybe...

MONICA

That's totally a yes.

I tell myself that I'm just excited about working on the Galactic Command Base, but it's hard to ignore the way my heart picks up speed whenever I think about seeing Luke after tonight's shift. I've been on one date with the man—and he has me twirling around and checking my phone often.

I choke on my laugh while typing out my message.

ME

I don't know why I thought asking you all for help would be a good idea.

MONICA

It wasn't.

NANCY

She's joking. We'll be serious now!

WINNY

Where was this support for me a few moments ago?

NANCY

I love you enough to think you deserve better.

WINNY

Than a hot Santa?

MONICA

Those two words can't exist in the same sentence.

WINNY

You didn't grow up watching cheesy holiday romance movies and it shows.

I tuck my phone into my pocket and finish getting ready for work. Today, I choose to spend a little more time on my appearance, going the extra mile to curl my hair, add some eyeliner, and swipe a bit of highlighter on the tops of my cheekbones. I even tear the tag off a new scrub set I bought for the season and throw it on.

Do I feel a little ridiculous for being this worked up over seeing Luke later? Yes, but oh well. If getting dolled up and wearing a new pair of scrubs makes me feel good about myself, then screw it. I don't have much to lose.

Except your heart.

I push the thought away and exit my bedroom. My mom's eyes brighten when they land on me, and she pauses the TV show she was watching to follow me into the kitchen.

"You look nice."

"Thanks." I open my lunchbox and start packing a few snacks.

"I like your new scrubs."

"Oh. Thank you." I self-consciously brush a hand down the front of the smooth material, ironing out a nonexistent wrinkle. My mother has never commented on my scrubs before, so I'm surprised she noticed a new set, let alone complimented it.

"You have a leftover piece of the plastic tag stuck in your hair."

Before I have an opportunity to search for it, my mom walks over and plucks the incriminating piece of evidence from my curled strands.

"There." She gives my shoulder a squeeze before adjusting my hair so it falls down my back. "You look beautiful."

"Because I decided to wear makeup today?" My eyes automatically roll. My mom is the type who encouraged us to never leave the house without makeup on and our hair done, so I'm not shocked at her approval.

"No." She shakes her head, stunning me. "Because you look *happy*."

My heart—that traitorous organ that can't seem to pull itself together lately—aches from her statement. I feel a bit like an asshole for assuming the worst, which is something I clearly have to work on if I ever expect our relationship to improve.

She's trying, so you should too.

Yet despite the mental reminder, I'm not sure how to respond to her. Thankfully, I don't have to as she pulls me into a hug, enveloping me in the scent of her floral perfume and the hint of cinnamon that clings to her clothes and hair during *coquito* season.

"I know things have been…hard for us, especially more recently." *That's putting it lightly.* "I'm sorry that I haven't been the easiest to get along with. I've spent some time thinking about what we talked about the other day, and there is truly nothing that makes me happier than to see *you* happy. If I ever made you believe otherwise, then I'm sorry, and I'll work to be better."

"Really?" I look at her while rapidly blinking my eyes as a precautionary measure against breaking into tears.

"Really." My mom kisses my cheek before exiting the kitchen, leaving me to wonder if maybe there is hope for our relationship after all.

Luke isn't waiting for me in the break room after our shifts are over like we had planned, so I make him and myself a cup of coffee before I wait at the same table we sat at last time. Time goes by painfully slowly, and after ten minutes, I battle between texting him or not. I don't want to seem desperate or clingy, so I consider taking his absence as a sign of maybe him getting held up with an emergency case.

I have this gut feeling that Luke wouldn't ditch me without letting me know, especially not after last night's kiss and him asking me out on another date. So, I muster up some courage and text him to check in.

ME

Hey. Your coffee is getting cold.

I send a photo of the cup I made him after I arrived because I wanted to keep my mind busy.

More like you wanted to do something nice for him. I groan under my breath at the thought before I wait for a response that never comes. Eventually, my message goes from delivered to read, and I sit with my stomach in knots while I wait for a response that never comes.

After ten more minutes of staring at my phone like it might combust, I dump out my half-finished coffee and Luke's untouched one before heading to the parking garage.

During my drive home, my negative thoughts get the better of me, and I'm already assuming the worst about our situation. I had hoped Luke would answer me at some point before I parked in front of my parents' house, but no text ever comes.

Is he having cold feet about us after last night?

Did he realize that I'm not worth the trouble since I'll be leaving anyway?

I can't escape the worried thoughts plaguing my head, and Luke not answering my message only fuels them. He should've responded to my text already, but maybe he doesn't want to talk anymore.

The thought of that happening makes my stomach sour, and I struggle to unwind once I get home. No matter what I do, I can't distract myself from being annoyed for caring so much about someone after one stupid date.

I told myself multiple times that I'm leaving come January first, so it would be in my best interest to keep to myself, but here I am, agonizing over whether or not a guy texts me.

That's because you're growing attached.

The realization hits me harder than I expected, and I'm not sure what to do with the information. With a traveling job like mine, becoming dependent on someone from Lake Wisteria isn't an option for me, especially not someone who could be a part of my life for the definite future because he is best friends with my future brother-in-law.

Maybe you should have thought about that before you agreed to a date.

Something about Luke made me want to try. Aiden never pushed to break through the protective barrier I kept in place, but it only took Luke a few occasions to make me question letting someone in.

Stupid mistake.

Today's situation proves why I should've stuck to my original plan to keep to myself and survive the month until I head out to California.

Instead of giving my pessimistic thoughts any more fuel to grow, I choose to focus on my future and check if the place I previously stayed at is available, because unlike Luke, me leaving for Los Angeles is a sure thing.

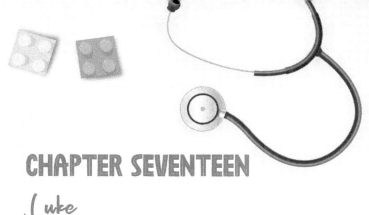

CHAPTER SEVENTEEN

Luke

Whenever I lose a patient, I always fall into the harmful pattern of punishing myself for not doing everything possible to help them. It isn't healthy or truthful, but I can't help it. I'm the doctor in charge of saving lives, so whenever I lose one, it feels like I failed not only them, but myself.

Losing people is an unfortunate but common part of emergency medicine, but regardless of how many times Aiden or other coworkers tell me that, every death hits me hard.

It's why I couldn't show face, despite telling Catalina I'd meet her after our shifts. I didn't want her to watch me spiral, so I pulled back. It's my perfectionism acting up again, and instead of letting her see my self-loathing and unrealistic standards I hold myself to, I shielded her from that side of myself.

I pull up the text thread for the

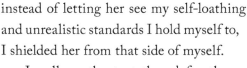

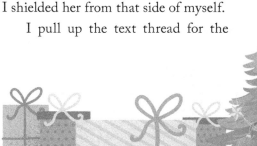

third time this afternoon, only to be disappointed when I read over the same text I sent an hour ago.

ME

I'm sorry for flaking. I got caught up with something at work and couldn't text you until later.

Catalina must still be asleep, so I distract myself until she texts me back hours later.

CATALINA

No problem. I understand.

ME

Are we still on for tonight?

She doesn't answer right away, so I spend the next thirty minutes panic-cleaning the apartment, preparing for the best-case scenario of Catalina coming over while anticipating the worst.

You shouldn't have stood her up. I've been kicking myself for the last hour about it, but there is nothing I can do to take my decision back.

My phone pings halfway through vacuuming the floor, so I turn it off and check my messages.

CATALINA

I don't think that's such a good idea.

ME

Why not?

I send my reply right away, not bothering with playing hard to get.

CATALINA

I'm not looking to be in a serious relationship right now.

With a disgruntled groan, I drop onto my couch and run my fingers through my hair while I consider Catalina's attitude shift. Obviously, I should've texted her yesterday instead of waiting until I was in a better headspace, but I didn't want her to see me at such a low, and now I'm stuck paying the price for my actions.

I knew she was skittish about all of this, and my decision didn't help matters.

ME

No one said anything about a serious relationship.

At least not aloud. Sure, I've thought about where things could go between us, but I also understand this could go nowhere.

CATALINA

Dates usually lead to more, and that isn't an option for us.

ME

Why the sudden change of heart?

CATALINA

I'm heading to Los Angeles after the wedding.

Fuck. I knew this would happen, but I'm still disappointed by the reminder.

ME

OKAY.

CATALINA

So we can agree this won't be going anywhere.

ME

I never said that.

CATALINA

Then what are you trying to say?

ME

That I'm sorry about last night.

I'll deal with her moving away later, once I have a better understanding of whatever this is between us first.

CATALINA

No need to apologize. This was never supposed to be serious.

There she goes again, diminishing whatever connection we are forming in an obvious attempt at self-preservation.

I'm not sure what changed in the time between our kiss on her porch and now, outside of the obvious issue of me blowing off our coffee date, but I'm not about to give up just because Catalina is back to creating distance.

> **ME**
>
> I'm sorry if I hurt your feelings by not showing up last night.

Her text is instantaneous.

CATALINA

I never said you did.

> **ME**
>
> No, but if I were in your shoes, I'd be annoyed and put off.

> **ME**
>
> And if it didn't hurt your feelings, please take it easy on me today and pretend it did?

CATALINA

Is this an ego thing?

> **ME**
>
> No. It's a self-conscious thing.

Might as well be forthcoming and hope for the best.

CATALINA

Fine. Maybe it bothered me a little bit.

CATALINA

A TINY little bit.

CATALINA

But it also scared me because I
realized I cared.

Her honesty is refreshing because it shows that I still have a fighting chance to win her over, so I decide to return her truthfulness with some vulnerability of my own.

ME

I'm sorry. I lost a patient last night.

Her reply takes two seconds.

CATALINA

I'm so sorry.

Another message pops up before I can reply.

CATALINA

I've had days like those, and they
truly are the worst, and nothing
anyone else says or does can
make it better.

I suck in a deep breath and reply.

ME

It hit me harder than I
expected. I wasn't in a good
headspace after it happened,
so I wasn't thinking straight.

Dots appear and disappear twice before a new message appears.

CATALINA

You'd think we'd be immune to the feeling by now. That we would have built some kind of emotional tolerance to it or something, but I feel like it's only gotten worse over the years.

I'm surprised at Catalina's openness with me, especially after what she said earlier about this not going anywhere.

ME

I'd rather feel for every patient I lose than not feel anything at all.

CATALINA

Me too.

CATALINA

Mourning their life feels like the least we can do.

ME

I knew you'd understand.

I take a deep breath before sending my next message.

ME

Do you forgive me for no-showing yesterday?

The dots flicker on the screen before a new message appears.

CATALINA

Yes. And now I feel bad for assuming the worst about you when you were clearly just going through a hard time.

I crack a smile while typing out my next text.

ME

Exactly how bad are
we talking here?

CATALINA

Not bad enough to go over
there.

ME

Okay.

ME

Is now an acceptable time to drop a
tragic backstory about my parents?

CATALINA

Only if you promise to include
alcohol with the trauma dump.

ME

Deal. I'll throw in some takeout
from your favorite sushi spot too.

ME

I'll even split a Dragon's
Breath roll with you.

CATALINA

That's masochistic.

ME

I prefer the term "romantic" since
they'll always remind me of you.

Nice, Luke. If you didn't scare her away before, you're about to do so right now with that stupid text.

CATALINA
I meant what I said about not looking for a relationship.

She might not be looking, but people change their minds all the time, especially when they see what they could have so long as they put their fears aside and embrace the unknown. It's just up to me to show her that I'm not going to back down because she expects me to.

ME
I'm just asking to hang out.

CATALINA
Alone.

ME
Afraid you won't be able to keep your hands off me without chaperones?

CATALINA
More like I'm afraid *you* won't be able to keep yours to yourself.

ME
How about this? I promise not to kiss you again.

CATALINA
Oh really?

ME

Sure.

Because the next time we do kiss, it's going to be because Catalina initiates it, not me. Giving her all the power to make the next move might be a risk, but I have a feeling it will pay off.

Fingers crossed.

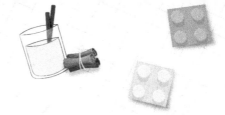

shake it before
you taste it

CHAPTER EIGHTEEN
Catalina

I swore to avoid Luke as much as possible after him not showing up, but then he texted me and explained his situation. Once he opened up to me about losing his patient, I couldn't hold his absence against him.

He brings out my sensitive side. A side that I've been cautious about exploring because I'm afraid of what I might uncover.

Terrified is more like it.

Despite my fears, I decide to hang out with Luke in his apartment anyway, obliterating my self-imposed vow to only see him at wedding events until I move away. I tell myself I'm only doing this out of pity, but deep down, I know it's more than that, although I refuse to acknowledge it.

We spend the first hour working on my speech while eating dinner before moving to the living room to work on the LEGO set. Aiden popped in to say goodbye before his shift at the

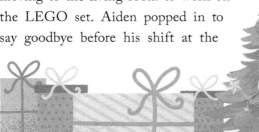

hospital and didn't bat an eye at the two of us hanging out, which makes me feel better about the situation.

Or as good as I can feel about being interested in a guy who I plan on leaving.

Spending time together feels like the most natural thing in the world, although it becomes progressively more difficult to ignore the growing sexual tension between us. My breath seems to hitch whenever I catch Luke looking at me, and a comfortable tingle rushes down my spine whenever our hands graze.

The reactions are uncontrollable, and they aren't anything I should feel embarrassed over, but that isn't my problem. It's the fact I'm already looking forward to the next time we can hang out, even if it's us meeting up in the break room at the hospital for some coffee.

Luke's eyes drop to my mouth for the third time in the last five minutes, and I wipe at the corners self-consciously. His brows pull together before he looks away.

"What?" I ask.

"Nothing."

"Sure about that?"

"Yes." A muscle in his jaw ticks.

"Doesn't look like nothing to me."

"I made a promise," he says with a low voice.

"Oh." My mouth falls open.

He wants to kiss you.

My heart thuds in my chest, the beats quickening as I remember the kiss we shared two nights ago.

"Disappointed?" he asks.

"Nope." I look away.

He leans in and presses his mouth against my ear. "I might have made a promise, but no one said *you* can't kiss *me*."

I shudder. "We shouldn't."

The tips of his fingers brush across my cheek before he tucks them beneath my chin. "Why are you fighting this?"

Because I'm scared.

Our eyes lock, and it seems like he reads my mind when he asks, "Is there anything I can do to make it easier?"

I exhale a shaky breath. "Just...give me time."

He drops a kiss on the top of my head before pulling away. "I can do that." He exhales. "Even if it might kill me in the process."

"Good thing I know CPR."

"Now that's one way to get you to kiss me."

We both break out into laughter, and I feel lighter because of it as we continue building the LEGO set. I ignore the yearning that builds inside me with every touch of our hands, which proves to be a difficult feat in itself.

Accepting we have a physical and emotional connection is one thing, but acting on it?

A mistake waiting to happen.

My mom enlisted the town's event coordinator, Josefina Lopez, to help her with planning the *parranda*. Josefina was excited by the idea, especially since our family hasn't done one since before my dad's mom, who always planned them, passed away. Gabriela isn't able to help because she is in full-on wedding mode, so I'm in charge of choosing songs for the event while my mom is busy helping coordinate everything else with Josefina.

The bus we rented for the night stops in front of my parents' house, and the crowd of *parranderos* on the lawn rushes toward the doors as they open. Josefina shuffles her grandson, Nicolas Lopez, onto the bus. She entrusted the young boy to help my dad play the *cuatro*.

"Ready?" Mami asks me while holding out a tambourine.

"Yup." I scan the crowd in search of one person who said he would be here.

I don't spot Luke's tall frame anywhere. Gabriela and Aiden are standing in line to get on the bus, but I don't see him beside them, so maybe he isn't showing up after all.

When I texted him earlier to remind him about the time and meet-up location, he answered with a "sounds good." If we didn't have an amazing time building his LEGO set last night, I would've spent the day overthinking his two-word reply, but maybe I should have.

"Cata!" my sister shouts from the front of the bus. "Let's go!"

With a parting glance toward the empty front yard, I head to the bus.

As the doors begin to shut behind me, someone knocks against the glass.

"Hey."

The doors part with a *whoosh*, and Luke steps onto the bus dressed in jeans, an unzipped black jacket, and a green sweater underneath that complements his pale skin.

His smile draws out one of my own.

"You made it," I say.

"I told you I would."

"Luke! Took you long enough!" Aiden calls from the back of the bus, where he and Gabriela saved us two seats.

"Did you really think I'd miss out on this?" He presses the palm of his hand against the small of my back and gently directs me down the aisle.

"When I didn't see you outside, I assumed something came up." I peek over my shoulder to find him grinning.

"Is that Catalina code for *you missed me*?"

I scoff at his comment.

"There's no place I'd rather be than here with you," he whispers in my ear, and my heart soars into dangerous, delusional territory.

I swore I'd be more careful around Luke and not get overly invested, but it's difficult when he says the sweetest comments and looks at me like I'm special. Like I mean something to him, even if I'm dead set on making sure I don't feel the same way about him.

Maybe Luke will get bored of the push and pull happening between us and give up, or maybe he really is determined to show me that letting someone like him into my life isn't such a bad thing, so long as I'm willing to let my guard down and give him a real chance.

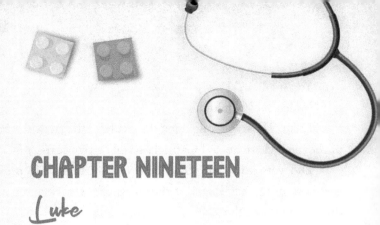

CHAPTER NINETEEN

Luke

When Catalina explained the concept of a *parranda* to me, I pictured it like a Christmas movie, with a small group of people stopping in front of houses to sing a few Christmas songs before walking to the next one.

The reality is far more exciting, and one I immediately find myself enjoying as everyone departs the bus and stands in front of the first house on the Martinezes' list of guests.

"*Parranderos!*" Mrs. Martinez waves her tambourine in the air. "Get your instruments here."

A crowd forms around Mrs. Martinez and Josefina Lopez while they pass out maracas, tambourines, and other noisemakers. I reach inside the basket and grab a maraca, which seems like a safe bet.

Mrs. Martinez gives my cheek a kiss before whispering, "Thank you for being here. My daughter might not tell you herself, but she's happy you came."

A warmth spreads through

me as I glance over at Catalina, Aiden, and Gabriela. They are talking amongst themselves, or more like Gabriela is animatedly telling a story, her hands waving in the air as she talks with them.

As if she senses me watching, Catalina glances over at me with a shy smile that beckons me forward.

Josefina stops me first, and I grab a music pamphlet from her hand before heading over to my friends.

Aiden throws his arm around Gabriela and drags her against his body, and I wish to do something similar with Catalina, but I resist the impulse. I'm not sure where we stand as far as PDA goes, and I'd rather not make tonight's fun activity awkward by attempting anything that makes her uneasy.

So, I hover close enough to smell her perfume while remaining far enough to look casual from an outsider's point of view.

Mrs. Martinez walks up the steps and asks, "Is everyone ready?"

The crowd forming near the entry of the house confirms with a shake of their instruments while a few people shout "yes!"

Catalina shifts her weight for the third time since I appeared, so I lean my head down and ask, "Are you feeling okay?"

She looks up at me. "Yes. I will be."

Will be.

"What's wrong?"

"I just get a little nervous with big crowds, but it'll go away."

"Anything I can do to help you feel better faster?"

She tucks a curl behind her ear, drawing my attention toward the holiday-inspired earrings she is wearing that look like miniature gift-wrapped presents. "Just...stay close?"

"How close are we talking?" I waggle my brows, making her laugh.

Out of the corner of my eye, I catch Aiden and Gabriela looking at us, along with a few other people based on the way the back of my neck prickles, but I ignore them all while I wait for Catalina's response.

She doesn't speak, but her hand reaching out to grab mine is the only one I need. Her hold is tight, most likely to disguise her trembling, so I readjust and grasp hers with a strong grip.

"Thank you," she says as we walk up the steps together toward the front door. For a moment, I panic, thinking Gabriela ruined my surprise for later.

"Thank you for what?"

"For being here. With me." She looks up at me with a dazzling smile that rivals all the twinkling lights covering the house in front of us, and I'm stunned by the sheer intensity of it.

Stunned by *her*.

I'm quickly learning that the next ten days won't be enough time for us, or at least not when a smile and a simple thank-you make me feel like I'm on cloud nine.

While I'm certain of my feelings, Catalina is the complete opposite, and I'm not sure where we will stand once it comes time for her to leave for her next job in California.

Focus on the present.

I'm trying my best, but what happens when the future I want is tied to the woman who is slowly drifting out of my reach?

We make it through four houses without any incidents, and our group of carolers has doubled in size since the very first stop. I try my best to sing in Spanish—*try* being the key word— and earn a few laughs from Catalina in the process. Despite the happiness shining in her eyes, there are a few moments when they turn cloudy from unshed tears, and I quickly figured out that her sadness is triggered by Nicolas Lopez playing the cuatro, which apparently used to be her grandmother's job before she passed away.

I can't do much besides wrap my arm around her and pull her into my side, offering my support in the only way I know how. My proximity seems to do the trick, and Catalina eventually seeks me out on her own.

I'm nervous but excited by the time we make it to the final house.

"No way!" Catalina rushes over to the table of snacks after the *parranderos* finish singing. "Gabriela! Look at this!"

Gaby flashes me a knowing smile before walking up to her sister. "*Tembleque*. Abuela and Papi's favorite." She grabs one of the small plastic cups and a mini spoon.

"Who made it?" Catalina asks.

I rub the back of my neck subconsciously before scolding myself for looking nervous. Aiden's mouth opens, but I shake my head to stop him from speaking.

"I wonder…" Gabriela does a shitty job at hiding the truth.

Catalina's gaze swings around the room. "Was it Mami?"

"No." Gabriela scoops a spoonful of the coconut pudding from the cup and takes a bite. "That's…um…" Her brows scrunch together.

Fuck. It's terrible, isn't it? I should've known Aiden was lying when he taste-tested the thing, but he swore to me that it was similar to the one he had when visiting Puerto Rico, so I believed him.

"What?" Catalina snatches a spoon from the table and tries a bite from her sister's cup. Her eyes widen, increasing my anxiety twofold.

Shit. Thank God I didn't tell anyone but Aiden and Gaby that I made the dessert or else I would've never lived the embarrassment down. I only bake for Aiden and myself, so bringing a dessert to an event?

Nerve-racking to say the least.

Catalina shocks me by stealing another spoonful of *tembleque* from her sister's cup before earning a slap on the wrist.

"Get your own," Gabriela hisses.

Catalina takes a bite with a smile. "Damn. That's so good."

Aiden shoots me a look and mouths, *I told you so.*

Huh. Maybe there is hope for me in the kitchen after all, so long as I stick to baking.

"You've got to try this." Catalina grabs my hand and pulls me toward the table. "It tastes exactly like my grandma's recipe."

My chest clenches at her statement. "I've heard."

"You have?"

Gabriela pops her head out from behind my back. "Yeah. I told him about it when he asked if he could bring anything for the *parranda*."

Catalina's eyes bounce between me, her sister, and the table. "Did you…"

Aiden claps a hand on my shoulder. "Luke woke up at the crack of dawn to start making it so it would have enough time to chill in the fridge."

Catalina's eyes widen. "You did?"

I resist the temptation to rub my neck, trying my best to ignore the prickling sensation. "Yeah."

She shakes her head in disbelief. "I had no idea you bake."

"I mess around sometimes."

Aiden's eyes roll. "By *mess around*, he means obsessively practicing a recipe until he finally believes it's good enough."

"I'm going to assume that means you use a scale?" Catalina looks up at me.

I fake an outraged scoff. "Is that even a question?"

Catalina places her cup on the table, pushes Aiden aside, and wraps her arms around my waist. "Thank you."

I hold her firmly against my chest. "You're welcome."

She tilts her head back so I can get a good look at her eyes. "When did you start baking?"

"Aiden's mom suggested trying it out to reduce stress— and turns out it works."

She lets out a soft laugh. "I'll take your word for it."

"I'm just glad what I made is edible. It's my first time trying out that particular recipe."

"It's more than edible. It's *amazing*." Her eyes light up. "My grandma would've loved it." She pulls away from my embrace all too soon. "I appreciate you going through the trouble of making it."

"See, I wanted to impress this girl…"

Aiden chokes on a laugh, and I elbow him in the ribs hard enough to make him stop.

"I have a feeling she is more than impressed."

"Are they flirting? It's hard to tell," Gabriela whispers loudly behind me.

"I'm starting to understand why Luke has spent the last couple of years single."

I flip him off, making someone nearby gasp.

Catalina flashes me a smile. "Do you want to go outside and get some air?"

"Hell yes."

Catalina ignores Aiden and Gabriela's commentary as she reaches for my hand and pulls me away from the crowd. I follow her out of the house and onto the warm, empty bus.

"Be honest with me. Was it really that good or—"

Catalina cuts my question off with a searing kiss that makes my breath hitch. One of her hands wraps around my neck, securing me while the other presses against my pounding heart.

I grip her hips to hold her in place while she unleashes a torrent of feelings. My desire grows with every pass of her tongue across mine, and my cock thickens in my pants as she presses her body against me. I swallow her groan and swivel my hips, and she tugs on my hair and sucks on my bottom lip in retribution.

It's a game of push and pull. Like a mental tug-of-war, wondering who will break first, taking the attraction we share to the next level. I'm not sure how long we stand there, exploring this growing connection between us, but I'm reluctant to stop.

Catalina is the one who pulls her mouth away first, but not before she plants one last soft kiss against my lips. I press my forehead against the top of her head in an attempt to shield my flushed face.

I'm not prepared to look at Catalina just yet. Not ready to scare her away with whatever emotions are clearly written across my face.

She brushes a hand down my shirt, smoothing the cotton material she wrinkled in her tight fist. "Why did you make *tembleque*?"

"Because Gabriela told me how much you liked it."

"What else did she say?"

I hesitate to answer.

Catalina draws invisible circles across my chest with the pad of her finger. "Your heart is beating fast."

"Because you make me nervous."

"Nervous?" She cracks a smile. "Me?"

"Yeah. *You*."

"Why?" she asks with a smile in her voice.

"Because you're you."

"And who am I exactly?"

The girl I can see myself falling for, even if she has no intention of falling with me.

"Someone special," I answer instead.

Her head tilts. "That's it?"

"Were you expecting some kind of love confession after only three dates?"

"Two," she corrects while holding two fingers up.

I grab her hand and kiss her palm. "I'm counting the double date with Gabriela and Aiden as one."

"Can it really be considered a date if I had no idea?"

"I think you put two-and-two together real fast."

Her eyes sparkle with amusement. "Doesn't make it an official one."

"It's not like I could've come out and asked you straight away to go out with me."

"I would've said no."

"Exactly."

She traces an invisible heart over the spot where mine beats rapidly in my chest. "But that doesn't mean I'm not open to another."

Her confession makes me elated. "Really?"

She rises on the tips of her toes, and her mouth hovers over mine. "But just one."

We'll see about that.

She seals her comment with a kiss, and goddammit, I know it'll never be enough with this girl. It's a gut feeling, and one that solidifies with every interaction we have.

It becomes clear to me that Catalina's time in Lake Wisteria might be coming to an end after her sister's wedding, but ours as a couple has just begun.

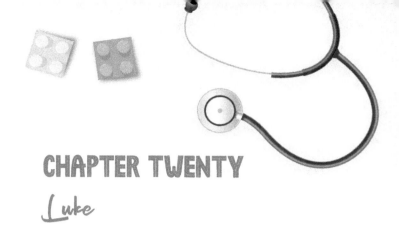

CHAPTER TWENTY

Luke

atalina and I fall into a pattern over the next few days of meeting up at work to write her speech, spending our free time together building the LEGO set, and texting during the in-between. I feel like I'm in high school again, constantly thinking of my crush and counting down the hours until I see her again.

I've been careful not to push Catalina too hard, so I usually wait for her to text me first, although I can't resist kissing and touching her as often as possible. We haven't gone any further than that, and the wait is driving me crazy, but I refuse to be the one to break first.

I want Catalina to be begging for me to touch her. To fuck her hard—

"What's got you smiling like that?" Aiden turns around. The man working on the hem of his tuxedo pants double-checks the length before asking him to step down.

"Nothing." I toss my phone on the couch and step onto the platform.

"Catalina?" He grins.

"Maybe."

"Has she invited you over for Christmas Eve?"

"Um. No."

"Huh."

I shake off the feeling of self-doubt. "It's fine. I was planning on spending the night watching a few classic movies and going to sleep early since I work the next day." Months ago, I happily volunteered to take Aiden's shift so he could spend the day with his and Gabriela's families, and now I'm grateful for the distraction.

The holidays are always hard. I hate being reminded of how different my relationship is with my parents compared to other people like Aiden, and regardless of how hard I push to connect with my parents, they don't reciprocate.

His frown deepens. "Seriously? Why don't you come over to the Martinezes' place with me? My parents are going to be there too since they're flying in a few days early for the wedding."

Usually, I spend the holidays with Aiden's family, but since they're spending it with the Martinezes, I feel more like a party crasher than a pseudo family member.

"Catalina and I might have gone on a couple of dates, but that feels a bit…serious."

He swallows a laugh.

"What?" I ask with a frown.

"Hate to break it to you, but based on the way you both

are acting with each other, I think things are already serious, don't you?"

"I don't know." We haven't defined what we are, and up until this point, I've been okay with it until Aiden opens his big mouth and asks a daunting question.

"So you haven't thought about a long-distance relationship?"

"I didn't say that." My teeth grind together.

"That's what I thought."

"There's no guarantee she will want one."

"No, there isn't, but I'm pretty sure she will be on board."

"Really?"

"Yeah. I've seen the way she looks at you."

I press my lips together to stop myself from pestering him for more information. Thankfully, Aiden shares his observation anyway when he says, "I've never seen her look at someone else like that, so whatever you're doing, keep it up."

My confidence grows from the compliment. "I want to take the next step, but I'm not sure how she will react."

Aiden shrugs. "You'll never know unless you try."

"What if it's a massive failure?"

"If there is anyone who can fix a problem like that, it's you, Captain America."

I salute him with my middle finger before promising to ask Catalina later tonight about Christmas.

I do not ask Catalina about Christmas because I never have a chance. She storms into the empty break room, looking like a hellion as she heads over to *our* table where I'm currently seated. She looks down at me with her hands on her hips and a fire burning in her eyes.

"You're planning on spending Christmas Eve *alone*?"

Thankfully, we're all alone or else I'd be embarrassed by the idea of someone knowing about my family situation.

I drag a hand through my hair. "Not exactly."

"That's not what Gabriela said earlier."

Fuck. Aiden really had to go open his big mouth and stir up some trouble because he didn't trust me to inconvenience the Martinez family on my own. I'm both annoyed at his perseverance and touched that he cares enough about me to want me around for the holidays.

But mostly, I'm annoyed, especially as Catalina scowls at me.

"I'm used to it."

"Well, prepare to get unused to it because you're not hanging out in your apartment, watching sad holiday movies by yourself while eating a frozen dinner."

I raise a brow. "One, Aiden promised to make me something, and two—"

She slices her hand through the air, cutting me off. "No."

"No?" I ask with a hint of amusement.

"I don't care what Aiden promised. I can't sit around my house and ignore the fact that you're all alone in yours."

I take a deep breath. "Why not?"

Her brows scrunch together as she bears a look of concentration. "What do you mean *why not*?"

"Why do you care if I'm all alone?"

She looks so damn determined in that moment. "Because

I like you."

The tension in my chest loosens as I smile. "You do?"

Her eyes roll. "Yes, but keep acting all pathetic, and I might change my mind."

I grab her hand and brush my lips across her knuckles. "Is that right?"

She visibly trembles.

"How can I make sure you don't change your mind?" I ask.

"Come over for Christmas Eve."

I give her hand a squeeze before releasing it. "Who knew you were so demanding?"

"You haven't seen anything yet." Her voice has a huskiness to it that wasn't present a few moments go.

"I look forward to finding out." I stand, drop a quick kiss on the top of her head, and escape the break room before I put my self-restraint to the test and fail miserably.

On Christmas Eve, I show up to the Martinez home armed with a decently priced bottle of wine and a batch of chocolate chip cookies I panic-baked to make up for not having any presents. Aiden stole one earlier and claimed they were nearly as good as the town's best bakery, Sweets & Treats, so that made me slightly more confident in my choice not to come empty-handed.

My idea seems to be the right decision when Catalina drags me inside with a smile on her face.

"You baked cookies?"

"Yeah."

"Keep this up and I might have to take you with me when I leave."

"I wish," I answer honestly.

Her eyes twinkle as she pulls me deeper into the house. The smells coming from the kitchen make my mouth water, and I'm tempted to go in there to check on what's for dinner, but Catalina doesn't stop walking until we enter the living room where everyone is spread out in array of holiday-themed clothes and accessories.

"Luke." Aiden's dad greets me with a clap on my shoulder and a one-armed embrace.

"We've missed you." His wife comes up to my side and plants a kiss on my cheek, staining it red with her lipstick.

Aiden's two siblings push their parents aside and hug me, making me feel more wanted in a single minute than I have by my parents all year.

Catalina disappears into the kitchen, leaving me to catch up with Aiden's family while the Martinezes and Aiden's dad prepare the table for dinner. We're then all shuffled into the small dining room, where mismatched chairs were added to the table to make room for all the new guests.

Catalina is quiet throughout dinner, which isn't unusual for her, although now I understand it comes from a place of shyness rather than a lack of care. I keep my thigh pressed against Catalina's at all times, and she seems to slowly loosen up as the conversation flows to happy subjects like Aiden and Gabriela's upcoming wedding.

"How's the speech coming along, Catalina?" Aiden's mom asks.

"Good." She looks up from her plate. "Luke has been helping me out."

"Oh really?" Aiden's dad glances over at me.

"Yup," I say with a tight throat.

"They've been working on it for over a week already," Aiden adds.

"I'm happy you found the time with your busy schedules." His mom grins.

"I've heard they've been working on it during their breaks at work," Gaby says with a knowing smirk.

"I had no idea you all were so invested in my schedule." Catalina's cheeks flush.

"Oh, it's not your schedule we care about." Aiden's mom waggles her brows.

Catalina wipes her face with a groan, making me laugh.

"I hope the Martinez family considers never inviting you troublemakers back for Christmas," I tease to get some of the attention off Catalina.

"Why? Hoping you get to keep them all to yourself next year?" Aiden's little shit of a brother asks.

"Max!" his mom whisper-shouts.

Max shrugs before inhaling a massive bite of pork.

If I'm invited back next year, I'll make sure Max isn't on the guest list because he's on my shit list now. That much I can promise if Catalina and I are dating by next year. It's a big *if*, but one I'll hold out hope for, so long as we survive a long-distance relationship.

Well, so long as I can get Catalina to agree to one first.

CHAPTER TWENTY-ONE

Catalina

O nce Aiden's family and mine move from the dining area
to the living room to exchange gifts, I head to my room
and return to the kitchen where Luke is loading the
dishwasher.

"I got you something." I'm so nervous, I toss Luke's present
in the air, forcing him to catch it instead of handing it over to
him like a normal person.

He stares at the gift like it's a ticking time bomb. "You got
me a present?"

"Uh, yeah?" My idea sounded good in theory, which is
why I drove to the closest big box store thirty minutes away to
pick it up earlier today. The place looked like a post-apocalyptic
movie, with endless barren shelves and a
sad group of toys that didn't make it onto
anyone's holiday wish list.

I was lucky to score the second-
to-last item on the shelf, although
it took me over twenty minutes to

find it since a kid hid it in the wrong aisle, most likely in hope of coming back to buy it later.

"I didn't get you anything." His brows pull together as he leans against the counter and holds the package in front of him.

"You made cookies."

He scoffs. "That's hardly a gift."

"Mine can barely be considered one, so don't feel bad."

"But—"

"Just open it and you'll see."

He rips at the wrapping paper with a smile that grows once he sees what is hidden underneath the gift wrap.

"A keychain?"

I reach over and point at the white coat the yellow LEGO is wearing. "He looks just like you."

He stares at it.

I can't stand the silence, so I speak again, "Now you'll always have it on you so you can remember you're not an imposter."

"That's..." He doesn't finish his sentence.

I nervously fidget with my headband, making the bells on the tips of my reindeer antlers jingle. "I told you it wasn't much of a gift."

"Thank you." He smiles, and I return it with one of my own as he pulls the keychain out of the box.

Luke reaches into his pocket for his car fob and immediately adds my present to the metal ring. It makes me excited to see him using my present already, especially since I spent the last few hours worrying that he would find it goofy.

He tosses his keys on the counter and wraps his arm around

my waist, tugging me against his chest. "I love it."

"It's not a lot—"

"It's *perfect*."

I fiddle with my earring, a nervous habit.

"Really. This might be the sweetest Christmas present someone has gotten for me in a long while."

"No way," I say in disbelief.

He lets me go. "I'm being serious. The last time I spent the holiday with my parents, they gave me an encyclopedia set."

"Are they big on reading?"

"Yes, their favorite genre is whatever can bore someone to death the fastest."

I laugh, which makes his whole face light up.

"They sound..." *Maybe you shouldn't finish that sentence.*

"I know exactly how they sound, and you're far too kind to say it aloud."

I fail to hide my wince. "I'm sorry."

"It's not your fault." He shrugs. The gesture should put my concerns at ease, but it only makes me feel worse about his home life.

"No, but that doesn't mean I can't feel bad on your behalf." I cup his cheek.

He leans into my palm, and I brush my thumb over his stubble. "Should I continue talking about them to earn more pity points?"

I poke him in the chest. "I don't pity you."

"Good, because trust me when I say I'm way happier spending the holiday with all of you anyway."

My heart skips a beat. "You are?"

He drops a kiss on the top of my head. "But mostly, I'm happy that I can be here with you." He hesitates before speaking again. "It means a lot that you invited me tonight." His next breath is shaky. "My parents… I try with them, you know? But it's pretty one-sided, and we don't really click. It doesn't help that I'm an only child, so it's not like I have siblings who help keep us all together."

"With them buying you encyclopedias for presents, it's hard to imagine why you don't get along."

He laughs, but it sounds more weary than happy. "I don't hold anything against them."

"You don't?"

"No. They could've been worse."

"A glowing endorsement as any."

His laugh sounds fuller this time. "I like when you get all protective of me."

"That's not—" My cheeks flush. "No. I'm…"

He leans in until our mouths are an inch apart. "You're *what*?"

I squint up at him. "I'm just annoyed they don't appreciate the person you are rather than the version they wish you would be." I'm not sure where the hell that came from, but I'm slightly embarrassed that I got that heated over people I've never met.

Thankfully, Luke saves me from self-doubt and rewards my confession with a kiss that makes my body melt into his.

"Well, there goes our plan to trick Luke and Cata into standing underneath the mistletoe," my sister says, loudly enough for half the house to hear.

Based on the gasps from the other room, everyone now knows about Luke and me.

As if they couldn't put it all together with the way you were both leaning into each other throughout dinner.

I pull away from Luke, only to have him plant the softest kiss on the corner of my mouth that quells some of my embarrassment.

I press my forehead against his chest. "How are we going to survive the rest of the week with them?"

His chest shakes beneath me from his silent laughter. "I have no idea."

"Is it too late to suggest that we skip the wedding?"

"*Para con eso*, Catalina Ana-Lucia Martinez-Rivera!" my sister shouts from the entryway.

"Keep embarrassing me and I will!"

"I'm hiding your passport and driver's license as we speak." Feet shuffling and the tinkling of jingle bells on Gabriela's hat follow her as she walks down the hall.

I tilt my head back to look Luke in the eyes. "Now what?"

"I'll follow your lead."

I shift my weight nervously from one foot to the other. "Meaning?"

"We can walk in there and pretend the last five minutes didn't just happen."

My heart dives into my stomach at the thought. "Or?"

"Or whatever you want. I'm open to suggestions."

"They're going to ask if we're officially dating."

His palm brushes my cheek before he cups it. "Is that a problem?"

Only because I don't know the answer. Calling Luke my boyfriend sounds…too serious. We've only been on a few dates. Sure, we've hung out quite a bit during the last two weeks, but that doesn't mean I'm ready for that next step.

Will you ever be ready?

After Aiden broke up with me, I was careful about the men I chose to casually date. It was *safe*. It meant not opening myself up to someone else until I was ready—and picking people who never pushed me out of that comfort zone to begin with.

While I'm not a hundred percent there yet, Luke has slowly started to dismantle my beliefs, replacing them with what-if scenarios.

What if I no longer punished myself for hurting my sister and allowed myself a chance at true happiness?

What if I stuck around Lake Wisteria for a little longer to see where things could go between Luke and me?

What if I stopped worrying about everything that could go wrong with dating my ex-boyfriend's best friend and embraced the possibility of falling in love with him instead?

Luke interrupts my spiral with a kiss to the top of my head. "Let's just go with the flow."

My face flushes. "You sure?"

"Yeah. We don't owe anyone any explanations."

I release a heavy exhale. "You're right."

I just need a little more time, I want to say but don't.

Don't give up on me just yet, I think but don't share aloud.

Show me that whatever we have is worth the fight, even if I doubt it, I beg without uttering a single word.

Luke's smile lacks its usual dose of sunshine, appearing far less confident than earlier as he leads me out of the kitchen. I ignore the pang in my chest and make a vow to myself to figure out what I want from all this before I leave Lake Wisteria again.

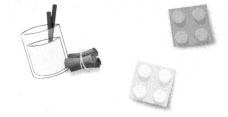

CHAPTER TWENTY-TWO

Catalina

uke and I spend the next few days balancing our work schedules, writing the maid of honor speech, and making some good progress on the LEGO set. I wish I could slow time down, but the days go by too quickly, and next thing I know, Gabriela and Aiden's big day is finally here.

While I'm happy for my sister, I'm counting down the hours until it's over. As the maid of honor, my duties are endless from the moment I wake up. Makeup and hair appointments. Countless photo-ops, first in matching robes, followed by our wedding outfits. A first-look photoshoot that had Gabriela ruining her makeup and left Aiden teary-eyed, which was both lovely and frustrating seeing as my sister needed to have her face retouched a few minutes before she was expected to walk down the aisle.

I haven't seen Luke yet, so when I find him waiting for me at the foot of the stairs, my heart skips a few beats. Yesterday, we practiced this same

routine of exiting the small building attached to the back of the church together. But when we rehearsed walking down the short outdoor path that leads to the front of the church, I wasn't nearly as nervous as I am now.

My knees shake at the sight of Luke standing before me, waiting to accompany me. I've seen Luke in scrubs, jeans, and a ridiculous elf costume that still makes me break out into laughter to this day, but him in a tux?

Damn. I'm struck with the urge to kiss him until we're both breathless, lipstick be damned.

"You look…" His darkening gaze travels down the length of me, making me shiver. "Absolutely stunning."

My knees go weak at the huskiness in his voice, and I wobble on my heels. I reach for the stair rail before I lose my balance and fall forward.

"You think so?"

"I won't be able to keep my eyes off you."

My cheeks warm under his hungry eyes. "You don't look too bad yourself."

He smooths out his lapels. "Less Captain America, more Batman today?"

I crack a smile. "Eh. I wouldn't go that far."

"You sure know how to compliment a man."

I take another step closer to him, making the icy blue material of my dress drag on the floor. "Would you rather I say what's really on my mind?"

"By all means."

"I'm thinking of every way I can get you *out* of that tux."

His devilish smile holds a secret promise. "Now I feel

better about my own thoughts then."

Heat blasts down my spine like invisible flames licking at my skin as I take the last few steps before stopping at the landing. Luke holds his arm out, and we lock elbows as he guides us toward the double doors that open up to the short walking path that wraps around the back of the church and ends right at the front where Gabriela will start her bridal march.

"I'm going to have a hard time keeping my hands to myself tonight," his husky whisper makes my lower half throb.

"Who said you have to?"

His brow arches. "Is that an invitation to do whatever I want?"

I nearly drop the small bouquet I'm holding. "Possibly."

"It's a yes-no question."

"Let's get through the ceremony and reception first," I say instead while readjusting my cashmere wrap so it covers as much of my exposed arms as possible.

He pulls my hand toward his mouth and kisses the back of it. "That's not the answer I was looking for."

I look up at him with a smile. "I'd rather keep you on your toes."

"You don't have to try too hard when you've got me wrapped around your little finger."

Butterflies burst inside me, turning my stomach into a giddy mess.

I'm not sure how I'll survive the next four hours in Luke's proximity while he looks at me like he is thinking of ten different ways to undress me, but I'm going to try my best for

Gabriela's sake. The last thing she needs is her maid of honor ditching the party early to go hook up with the best man.

But that won't stop me from counting down the minutes until I can.

I'm a ball of nerves as I rise from my seat in the reception hall and walk toward the mic. Luke's speech left the crowd laughing, as to be expected given his well-timed jokes and expertly crafted lines, so I'm only feeling added pressure to do well.

I walk over to Luke, who covers the mic with the palm of his hand before leaning over to press his mouth against my ear.

"You got this."

"I'm so freaking anxious," I say with a tense smile.

"Just picture me naked." He winks before helping me adjust the mic stand. "It'll make me feel less guilty about doing the same while you're up here."

My mouth falls open as Luke passes me a glass of champagne for the toast. His comment flusters me so much, I forget about how worried I am. Sexually frustrated, yes, but equally thankful, nonetheless.

With a smile, he heads back to his seat beside my empty one.

I clear my throat before pulling out my cellphone, opening my note-taking app, and turning to my sister and Aiden, who sit at a table facing the rest of the reception hall. Gabriela waves at me with a smile, and I return it with one of my own before facing the tables full of wedding guests.

"To those of you who don't know me, that was most likely intentional on my part, so allow me to introduce myself as Catalina, the antisocial Martinez sister—or to Aiden's family, the ex-girlfriend who still gets to enjoy his home-cooked meals without ever having to marry him."

Gabriela's cackling laugh filters through the air, making half of us break out into laughter as well, thus building my confidence.

I glance over at Luke, who leans back in his chair with his arms crossed. He looks at me like I'm the only person in the room, and damn, I'm tempted to ditch the reception and sneak out with him instead.

Someone coughs, stealing my attention away from the man who always seems to capture it.

You can do this.

"I'm not one for long speeches—or social gatherings for that matter—so I'll keep this short."

A few people clap before they're shushed by the crowd.

"When Gabriela and my parents taught us that 'sharing is caring,' I don't think they had boyfriends in mind." More people laugh this time, and some of the tension in my shoulders loosens. "I should've guessed it was a possibility given how my sister always stole my Ken dolls, but my parents said she would grow out of that phase…or so we thought."

Thankfully, more people laugh this time.

"Anyone who knows Aiden understands why Gabriela would fall in love with him. In fact, I'm the first one to admit that she has impeccable taste." I look over at her and wink, and Gabriela's smile widens.

"See, my sister has dreamed of meeting her prince charming ever since she was a little girl who forced me into wearing our father's suit for our pretend weddings while drawing a mustache across my upper lip with a Sharpie." The group of women near the back of the room gasp. "I *know*. To think, people call her the nice Martinez sister when she single-handedly gave me a permanent mustache during picture week."

"I thought it was a washable marker!" my sister shouts.

"So you say…" A wave of chuckles follows my comment. "Anyway, Gabriela had this stage where she was obsessed with weddings. She would watch the video of our parents getting married like it was her favorite movie, pointing out everything she loved about their special day. The flowers. The big, puffy dress. Our father waiting at the end of the aisle for his 'princess' as she put it.

"But little by little, as Gabriela got older, her view on weddings and husbands matured. It wasn't about the event, but rather the person she pictured standing at the end of the aisle. The man who would stick by her through the good and the bad. For richer and for poorer. In sickness and in health." My eyes sting, and I'm surprised I've held off on crying up until now. I avoid locking eyes with my sister, who is sniffling loudly behind me, solely because I know that one glance at her and my tears will never stop flowing.

On the one hand, I'm so happy for her, but on the other, I yearn for a love like hers. A love that might not be perfect, but one that will stand the test of time and all the trials that life brings our way.

I sneak another look in Luke's direction and catch the

proud smile on his face.

You got this, he mouths, flooding me with enough confidence to continue despite the ache in my chest.

I take a deep breath to gather myself. "My sister always knew what she wanted, which is why nothing made me happier than the moment she realized Aiden was the man who she saw herself sharing a life with."

Silverware clangs against water goblets and wineglasses again.

"The two of them are incredible people in their own right, but together? They're the power couple we all aspire to be, and I can't imagine two people better suited for each other. They make me believe that there is always room for love in our lives, so long as we are open to accepting the kind we think we deserve."

I turn to face my brother-in-law.

"Aiden, you embody everything my father is to my mother, which is exactly what my sister wanted and more, so thank you for loving her as much as we do and then some. We're happy to have you as part of our family, and I speak for every Martinez-Rivera here tonight when I say that we look forward to seeing your own family grow, along with your love for Gabriela. Congratulations, you two. I love you both more than words can express. Cheers." I hold up my glass of champagne.

My heart pounds in my ears, so I can hardly make out the sound of everyone clapping for me as I take a step away from the mic. My whole face warms up from hundreds of eyes on me, and I wish I could slink into the shadows. The DJ plays music, drowning out the sound of my heels clicking against the dance floor as I head back to my seat beside Luke's.

"Be honest with me. How did I do?"

Luke drags my chair closer to his until our legs touch. "Amazing." He pushes my wineglass into my trembling hand. "You were perfect up there and didn't mess up once."

"I heard some laughs."

"And a few sniffles."

"I'm sure my mom will give me a speech later about making my sister cry."

"And *Aiden*."

I push his shoulder with a laugh. "No way."

"You didn't see him discreetly dabbing at his eyes with the cloth napkin?"

"No. I tried to avoid looking at them directly."

"Hopefully, the videographer recorded it so I can save it as his contact photo."

I swallow my laugh. "So it went well you think?"

He tucks a loose strand of hair behind my ear. "Yes, except I'm curious about that new part you added."

My brows crinkle together. "What new part?"

"That they made you believe in love."

"Oh. Right." I look everywhere but his face. "It was a last-minute addition." And clearly a stupid one based on the way he is looking at me.

His face remains unreadable as he nods. "I noticed."

"Was it too sappy?" I don't let him answer before saying, "Yeah. Definitely cheesy. Ugh." I wrinkle my nose. "I should've run it by you first before embarrassing myself up there—"

He cuts my rambling off with a fierce kiss that does the

trick of shutting me up.

"Did you mean it?" he asks after pulling away.

"Mean what?" I blink up at him, too dazed to follow his line of thinking.

"That *there is always room for love in our lives, so long as we are open to accepting the kind we think we deserve*," he directly quotes my speech without missing a single word.

His intense gaze has me staring down at my lap. "I think so."

I've had my share of boyfriends in the past, including Aiden, but after him, I stopped trying to find someone good enough to marry one day. I've told myself countless times that I stuck to casual flings and guys who weren't interested in anything serious because it felt safe. I knew what I was getting myself into, so there was no risk of getting hurt or worse, hurting someone else.

Thinking back on it, maybe I picked people who were strictly casual because I didn't think I *deserved* the kind of love my sister and her now-husband have. After all, I was the reason they couldn't be together in the first place.

My poor life choices caused my sister to suffer and keep her feelings about Aiden to herself, so I decided that she was the one who deserved her happy ending with the guy of her dreams while I punished myself for being so damn selfish and oblivious to everyone else's feelings. But in the process, I was ignoring my own needs, wants, and dreams.

My sister wouldn't want me to hurt myself like this. She'd love for me to be happy too, and it's time I consider what that looks like. What my life could be like, should I let go of my self-sabotaging habits first.

Luke seems to read my mind as he asks, "What kind of love do you think you deserve then?"

"I'm not sure," I answer honestly, my voice small and hardly audible over the music streaming from the speakers.

He clasps my chin between his fingers and looks me in the eyes as he says, "Then it's up to us to figure it out. *Together.*"

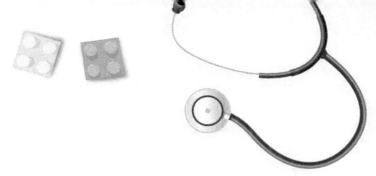

CHAPTER TWENTY-THREE

Luke

I've been told I'm a patient man, but my ability to control myself went out the window the moment Catalina appeared today, wearing a smile solely meant for me and a silk dress that highlighted every curve I've spent the last few weeks dreaming of.

Throughout the wedding, I couldn't keep my eyes off her, and I stole glances every chance I got. The groomsmen gave me shit about it, but I ignored them, knowing their teasing came from a place of envy. Because who the hell wouldn't be envious of whatever man is on the receiving end of Catalina's attention?

Hell, I'm envious of people who are her damn family, especially when her uncles and cousins whisk her away for a dance or two, leaving me to stew in the corner, nursing a beer, while I wait for my turn again.

Tonight has been a true test of my self-restraint, and I've done a

wonderful job. The challenge proves even more difficult once Catalina drags me onto the dance floor to the sound of the Martinez-Rivera family getting excited over whatever popular Latin song began streaming from the speakers.

"Just follow my steps." She places one of my hands on her hip while she grabs the other.

I let her take the lead, and she shows me how to properly dance to the music her family loves. All of them slap me on the shoulder and say a few words of encouragement, and after several songs, I get the hang of some basic moves.

Thankfully, Catalina is patient with me, never getting frustrated despite me stepping on her toes multiple times. She shows me how to shimmy my hips and smoothly spin her around until I can do it without her instruction, and I get her to laugh multiple times when I accidentally lose my rhythm.

I swear I haven't felt this level of contentment before, and it's all because of the dazzling woman in front of me, who seems to glow as she shares a story about how her dad never danced at parties until her mom showed up at one and started dancing with all the men except for him.

I relate to her father in this moment because before tonight, I was always comfortable sipping a drink in a corner while everyone else was on the dance floor.

Just another thing to add to my growing list of reasons why the thing I have with Catalina is special.

We continue dancing together until the DJ announces the last dance for the bride and groom. I'm reluctant to let Catalina go and end the spell between us, so I hold her hand and don't let it go throughout Aiden and Gaby's final dance and sparkler send-off.

I only release her when she needs to get inside the car I ordered to drive us back to town.

As I open the door for her, I say, "I'm going to have him drop you off first."

She doesn't reply as she slides into the back seat, and I follow behind her and close the door behind me. Before I have a chance to reach for her hand again, she grabs mine and interlaces our fingers first, making me bite back a smile.

"*Or* we could head back to your place." She keeps her voice low while peeking up at the rearview mirror.

I turn in my seat to face her. "We've both been drinking."

She shoots me an exasperated look. "I don't know about you, but I stopped feeling buzzed an hour ago."

"Same."

"But if you don't want to…" She sucks on her bottom lip.

Hell yeah, I want to. I shut her worries down with a kiss before telling our driver about the change of plans. The short ride to my apartment feels like a four-hour one, and I spend every second thinking of what I plan on doing with Catalina once I get her inside.

Perhaps I should tie her up so she can't leave for California in two days.

Now that's an idea.

"Luke?" Catalina calls.

"Huh?" I snap out of my thoughts.

"We're here." She flashes me a timid smile, and I hop out of the car so I can open her door before the driver has a chance.

My long steps are difficult for Catalina to keep up with in

high heels, so I end up tossing her over my shoulder to save her the trouble.

"Hey!" She laughs while smacking my back.

"You're too slow."

"Well, excuse me for not wanting to twist an ankle before we ever make it inside."

"An unnecessary risk when you have me."

She stops beating against my back and ass as I carry her up the small walk-up and into my apartment. I reach into my pocket for my keys and unlock the front door while the LEGO figure Catalina got me for Christmas spins around from the jerky movements, making me smile in the process.

The second I shut the door and place Catalina on her feet, she throws herself at me. Her lips crash against mine, and her nails dig into the front of my coat as she pushes me against the door.

Whatever thoughts I had disappear until I'm left with only one prerogative.

Making Catalina mine.

She seems to have the same idea as she yanks my coat off before chucking hers in the direction of the couch.

"Fuck." I shiver when she kisses a path down the column of my throat, and my head drops back to give her more room. The grip I have on her hips is punishing as she rolls them, pushing her center against my straining cock.

"I like the sounds you make," she says against my skin between kisses.

I reach around her, grab her ass, and lift her off her feet. She wraps her legs instinctively around my waist and returns to kissing me while I fumble my way through the dark, tripping over a few random belongings in the process of getting to my bedroom.

"Tell me this isn't a terrible idea," she says right before she lets out a shriek when I toss her on the bed.

Catalina bounces once before slamming back down on the mattress, and I take advantage of her breathless state to crawl over her body and seal my mouth over hers, gripping her chin tightly between my fingers while my tongue lashes out.

She returns my kiss with vigor, and it takes an incredible amount of self-control to pull away.

"Does this feel terrible to you?" I ask before sucking on her bottom lip. "Or this?" I brush my hand up the side of her body and give her breast a squeeze. She sucks in a breath when I tug on the bow holding her dress up and seal my mouth over her nipple, teasing her until she is trembling beneath me, begging for me to do something about the growing problem between her legs.

"Answer me." I suck on her skin until a mark starts to bloom.

"No."

"No what?"

"No, this feels right."

"We can do better than that." I steal another kiss from her, although this one borders on punishing before I focus on her other, neglected breast.

"Luke," Catalina groans my name as I swivel my hips and press my hard length against her center. She parts her legs, giving me room to worship her body like I've been dreaming of all night.

Hell, all *week*.

Despite my eagerness, I focus on calming down and taking my time to familiarize myself with Catalina's body. Studying what makes her sigh and groan and curse up at the ceiling as an overwhelming amount of pleasure courses through her.

I don't know how long I spend kissing, licking, and teasing her until she is writhing beneath me, begging for release, but I don't stop until she tugs on my hair hard enough to yank a few strands free.

"*Lucas*." Her nickname earns her a hard suck on her clit.

"Say my name."

"Fuck me first and maybe I'll remember it."

"Wrong answer." I deny the one thing she has been begging for and sink a finger inside her instead. The feel of her...the sounds she makes. It has my cock stiffen until I'm pressing into the mattress for some kind of relief.

She fidgets on the bed with a groan as I add a second one, earning a frustrated huff from her when I brush my thumb across her sensitive clit.

Catalina curls her fist around my comforter, her muscles tight as she trembles underneath me. With a few more slow pumps of my fingers, I drag myself away from the bed so I can ditch my clothes and grab a condom from my nightstand.

Catalina distracts me as she rolls over and reaches for my cock. Her hand wraps around it, and she tugs until I step closer to the edge of the bed. My vision turns hazy as she collects a drop of arousal leaking from the tip before tracing lazy lines down my hard length with her tongue. My legs feel like they might give out when she takes me into her mouth, and I have to reach for the nightstand to stop myself from sinking deeper.

"Shit." I consider pulling away, but she grips my ass and sucks hard enough to have me seeing stars.

"Catalina," I moan her name. "Fuck."

Her eyes flutter shut as she swallows around me. If she keeps this up, I'll come before I ever have a chance to end up between her thighs, and that thought alone stirs me into action.

It takes all my willpower to pull out of her mouth, and she makes a disgruntled noise when I step away from her.

I make quick work of the condom, add some lube, and clean my hand with a tissue before I return to the bed. Catalina stares up at me with hooded eyes as she spreads her legs, beckoning me forward. I grab a pillow and shove it under her ass before leaning forward to capture her lips with mine.

Her legs wrap around my waist, and she's the one to reach between us and lead me toward her center.

I press my forehead against hers. "There's no turning back if we do this."

"Already having regrets?"

"No." *But you might.* I banish the thought and any other doubts I have about our circumstance.

"Good," she says with a small smile as her heels dig into my spine.

My body trembles as I press into her. I slowly sink inside, teasing her with every shallow thrust of my hips. She gives up on being patient and meets my next thrust with her own, the jerky movement as harsh as her nails digging into my back.

We both let out a content sigh when I'm fully seated inside

her, and I'm tempted to stay this way until she shimmies beneath me and begs me to continue.

I kiss her jaw. Her cheeks. The top of her head and this sensitive spot on her neck that makes her back arch into me while I pump my hips. I'm slow at first, but my movements gain intensity as I drive into her harder. *Deeper.* At some point, she needs to press her palms against the headboard to keep in place while I fuck her.

She calls my name, and I soak the sound up, along with every moan that escapes her. Her nails drag against my back. My ass. My chest where sweat begins to bead underneath the smattering of hair covering my pecks.

Time ceases to exist in our lust-fueled bubble, and I want to make it last for as long as possible. Want to make the most of the night in as many positions as we can manage before I come.

When I feel myself getting close to the edge after Catalina comes with a cry, I pull out and flip her over, grabbing her by the hips and taking her from behind. This position is like heaven and hell all at once, because nothing that feels this good should ever come to an end.

Her cries feed the impulse to make her come again, and I reach around and play with her clit until she spasms around my cock once more.

She glances over her shoulder, and the look of pure bliss on her face—a look that exists because of *me*—sends me over the edge, and I throw my head back with a curse as I come.

When I return to reality after my blissful high, I pull out and turn Catalina around. She opens her arms, and I lie on top of her and trap her in my embrace, soaking in the smell of her perfume and the erratic beat of her heart while she brushes her fingers through my hair.

I'm reluctant to get up and toss the condom out in the bathroom, but I eventually force myself to leave the bed once I notice myself drifting into unconsciousness.

When I come back, Catalina is battling to keep her eyes open, so I help her into one of my T-shirts before tucking her underneath the covers. I slide in too and get settled behind her.

With my arm wrapped around her waist and my leg twisted with hers, I quickly fall asleep, knowing that come tomorrow, everything between us will have changed.

shake it before
you taste it

CHAPTER TWENTY-FOUR

Catalina

I wake up the next morning in a bed that isn't mine, beside a man who, only a few hours ago, was drawing every ounce of pleasure from my body. I'm not sure how late Luke and I stayed up, but it was worth the sleep deprivation and soreness that plagues me as soon as I peel my eyes open.

The spot between my thighs throbs at a particular memory of him laid out beneath me, his hands firmly gripping my hips while I rode him, and I wiggle in place to ease the ache.

Luke's arm clamps around me and drags me back against his firm, warm chest until my ass is pressing against his hard cock.

"Good morning." His lips brush over the back of my head as his thumb brushes back and forth over my hipbone.

"Morning," I drawl, my voice raspy from overuse.

"How'd you sleep?"

"Too good."

His chuckle makes my stomach explode with butterflies. "Is there such a thing?"

"Only when we're both expected to be at brunch in… What time is it?" I search the room for a clock and come up empty.

With a groan, Luke rolls out of bed in search of his phone. "Eight."

I release a sigh. "There's still time."

He crawls over my body and cradles my face between his hands. "I like the way you think."

I bat at his chest with a laugh. "I meant to get ready."

His eyes glitter as he juts his hips forward, pushing his erection into me. "Don't leave just yet."

"You're starting to get clingy."

He brushes his lips over mine. "You haven't seen anything yet."

"Is that a warning?"

"More like a promise of what's to come." He peppers my skin with kisses that leave my skin flushed and my core aching for some relief.

Luke makes quick work of the shirt he dressed me in last night, and it falls to the floor along with the boxer briefs he threw on before falling asleep.

We spend the next hour in bed, swapping kisses and orgasms until we're both tempted to fall back asleep. It takes every ounce of willpower I have left, which isn't much to begin with, to pull away from Luke's embrace and search for my maid of honor dress.

I cringe at the icy blue dress and all the wrinkles. The moment my parents see me returning to the house dressed like this, they'll know all about how I spent the rest of my night.

Shit.

Luke stretches across the mattress. "I bet your sister has some clothes stashed in Aiden's room."

"Oh my God. You're a genius!" I kiss his stubbled cheek before texting my sister in a rush to ask if she has anything I can borrow. Surprisingly, she answers right away.

GABRIELA
YOU STAYED OVER?

ME
Yes.

GABRIELA
Oh my God. You need to tell me everything!

ME
Can it wait until later?

GABRIELA
Are you kidding? I've been waiting for this.

ME
That doesn't sound creepy whatsoever.

GABRIELA
You know I'm a romantic.

ME
Yeah, a hopeless one who is looking too much into this.

The text feels like a lie, but I'm not about to get my sister's hopes up over something I'm still uncertain about.

Thankfully, Gabriela only follows up with an eye roll emoji before letting me know where to find her spare clothes.

ME

You're a lifesaver!

GABRIELA

I expect a full report while we get ready for the New Year's Eve party.

I ignore her text and hop in the guest shower, scrubbing my skin with a soap that smells exactly like Luke before throwing on a sweater and a pair of jeans my sister left here. Her boots are a little tight, but I'd rather wear them than my heels from last night.

When I walk out of the bathroom, I find Luke sitting at the breakfast nook, sipping on his coffee while scrolling through his phone. He looks up, and our eyes lock before a shiver skates down my spine.

"Keep looking at me like that and I'm taking you back to bed," he says with a hoarse voice.

I all but skip over to the table and take a seat beside him. "Thanks for this," I say before taking a sip of the coffee he made me.

He kisses the corner of my mouth, and my toes curl despite the limited space in my sister's boots.

We spend the next twenty minutes talking about the wedding while drinking our coffee and eating some leftover bagels from yesterday morning. It feels like a normal part of our routine. Like we always wake up every morning together, swapping stories and sharing laughs despite never having done this before.

It makes me feel *whole*, so when Luke is the one to remind us of our brunch plans, I'm hesitant to leave our little bubble.

"You're always welcome to stay the night again." He grabs my coat from the couch and helps me into it.

"I might take you up on that." I flash him a smile.

I thought sex would complicate matters, but if anything, it clarified my biggest worry.

Luke and I have a chemistry that can't be ignored, and no amount of avoiding it will make it disappear. And after last night, that's the last thing I want.

That much I know.

Luke and I are seated at opposite ends of the table for Catalina and Aiden's celebratory brunch, so I don't get a chance to talk to him again before I'm carted away with the bridal party to get ready for tonight's New Year's Eve bash at a bar in town called Last Call.

My sister's second-favorite holiday is New Year's Eve because she loves fireworks and gets all sentimental about new beginnings, so I can't think of a better way for her to spend her first day as a wife than celebrating the holiday amongst family and friends.

As soon as we make it to the rental house Gabriela and Aiden booked for their wedding weekend, my sister holds true to her earlier promise and pesters me with questions about Luke, all while her bridesmaids listen in like we're on a talk show.

Gabriela drops onto the couch beside me. "So..."

"Yes?"

"You and Luke."

"Mm." I nearly stab my eye with my mascara wand.

"Are you going to do the long-distance thing?"

I stare at her for a few moments. "Why are you asking?"

"If I didn't, that would make me a terrible sister."

"Terrible? Or respectful of my privacy?"

She tosses a throw pillow directly at my head. I dodge it, and it lands with a thud near one of her bridesmaids, who accidentally messes up her winged liner.

"Sorry!" Gabriela waves her hand with a laugh.

My hopes of my sister dropping the subject are dashed when she asks another question.

"How was it?"

"What?"

"The *sex*."

I glare at her. "I'm not talking about that with you."

She falls back against the couch with a sigh. "Okay. Fair enough, but will you at least update me on what's next for you two?"

"Nope."

"Cata!"

"That's none of your business."

"Well, this is me making it my business."

"Why?"

"Because I care about you and want you to be happy!"

I shoot her a scathing look that quickly melts away at the sight of her smile.

"*And* because I'm super nosy."

I bite back a groan. "I'm well aware of that." Growing up with a little sister taught me as much, although I know her curiosity comes from a place of love as well.

"Just tell me one thing," she says, her tone switching from giddy to serious.

I sigh. "What?"

"Does he make you happy?"

I don't hesitate to reply. "Yes. Very much so."

I'm not aware that I'm smiling until my sister returns mine with one of her own. "Good. Then that's all that matters to me."

A tight ball forms in my chest, surrounding my heart until it aches. "Now, are you going to get ready for tonight? Or are you going to keep hounding me with questions about my love life?"

"Does that mean you have a love life now?" She waggles her brows.

"Gabriela!"

She points an accusatory finger at me. "It's not my fault you walked right into that one."

"And now I'm the one walking away." I get up and use the restroom, hoping it ends the conversation before my sister is able to pry any more information from me.

I might not have everything with Luke figured out, but that's a discussion I need to have with him first. One that we will no longer be able to avoid come tomorrow because I'll be heading to California for my next job. A job which had once made me excited now makes me feel heavy, and there is nothing I can do about it.

CHAPTER TWENTY-FIVE

Luke

After brunch, Aiden heads back to our apartment to get ready for tonight's New Year's Eve party. I spend the next couple of hours helping him pack a few moving boxes while asking him questions about yesterday.

"Enough about me," he says, and I sigh. "What about you and Catalina?" Aiden drops the packing tape on his bed.

"What about us?"

"Come on, man. I know she was here last night."

My cheeks flush. "Then you know all there is to it."

"Have you talked to her yet?"

"About what?"

"That you want to do long-distance?"

"Um, no."

He stares at me with a gaping mouth.

"What?" I ask with a hint of agitation.

"Doesn't she leave tomorrow?"

"Yes." My teeth grind at the thought. I've tried my best to forget about Catalina's impending departure but it's impossible with the reality of our situation hanging over me and every decision I've made over the last twenty-four hours.

"And you haven't gotten around to bringing it up yet?"

I take a seat on the edge of his bed. "I didn't want to spook her."

"Now's not the time to worry about that." He starts to pace the floor, being mindful of the half-full boxes.

"I plan on talking to her about it."

"When?"

"Tonight." I speak with more confidence than I feel. New Year's Eve might not be the ideal setting for a serious conversation, but there is no way I can watch her leave tomorrow without her knowing where I stand.

He pinches the bridge of his nose with a sigh.

"I don't have an option. Either I talk to her about it tonight or wait until she heads out to California, and the more I think about that happening, the less I like it."

"You really like her."

Fuck yeah, I do. Last night further solidified my growing feelings toward her, and today pretty much made them concrete. I knew from the moment I started missing her only thirty minutes after she left with her sister and the bridal party that I was screwed.

I don't know how I'll survive her being gone, but I do know that I plan on using every tactic known to man to get Catalina to come back to Lake Wisteria, even if it means playing dirty to make it happen.

I'm instantly aware of Catalina's presence the moment she walks into Last Call. Everything around me fades as she steps inside the bar, looking heaven-sent with her golden dress that complements her skin tone and brown eyes.

I'm caught staring, a fact I don't try to hide as Catalina makes her way over to me and kisses my cheek.

"Miss me?" Her smile borders on timid, so I boost her confidence with a press of my lips against hers.

"From the moment you left."

"Sure you did." Her eyes roll, giving me a quick glimpse of her shimmery eye makeup.

"It's true. I'm afraid I'll struggle with a serious relapse episode when you move away."

"Is this your ploy to have me stay in Lake Wisteria?"

"Depends. Is it working?"

She laughs. "No, but I do enjoy the effort."

I loop my arm around her and signal for the bartender. Catalina orders a vodka tonic while I stick to the beer I was already drinking, resolute in my decision to not drink much tonight. If it's our last one together for a while, I want to make the most of it, and I need a clear mind for all the things I have planned.

"I could take a few days off and visit you," I stupidly say without any context.

Her brows pinch together. "What?"

"Sorry. I was thinking aloud."

She smiles around her straw. "About coming to visit me?"

"Yes."

"Can you take that many days off work?"

"Aiden owes me a few."

She brushes a hand down my button-down shirt. "And you'd use the favor on me? Why?"

"If you're still seriously asking me that, then we have an issue."

Her eyes glimmer. "Is that right?"

"Yes, because that means I've done a terrible job making my intentions clear."

Her smile expands. "The absolute worst."

I shake my head while fighting a smile. "Obviously, I need to be clearer."

"By all means, go ahead."

I cradle her cheek, making her suck in a breath before leaning my head forward. "I want you any way I can have you."

She tilts her head back to look me in the eyes. "Even if it means making long-distance work?"

"Don't they say distance makes the heart grow fonder?"

"It also makes it sadder." Her eyes soften at the corners.

"That's true, but three months will be over with before you know it."

"What about after?"

"No need to worry about that." If things go my way, and I'm certain I won't rest until they do, then Catalina will be coming straight home to me.

And I'll be counting down the days until then.

The group surrounding us shouts as the projector screen shows Times Square and the countdown clock that is about to hit sixty seconds before midnight.

"Cata!" Gaby pushes through the crowd with Aiden on her heels.

"Over here!" Catalina waves at them.

Gaby pulls her sister into a quick hug before Aiden wraps his arms around his wife as the timer gets closer to midnight.

"Ten…nine…"

My heart pounds faster with each number that is being chanted throughout the room, and excitement courses through my body at the thought of celebrating the new year with the woman beside me.

I curl my arm around Catalina's waist, and she looks up at me with a warm smile.

"Six…five…"

Her gaze drops to my mouth as she says, "Four…three…"

"Two…" I secure her in place by the back of her neck, and my thumb traces over her pulse point.

"Happy New Year!" The crowd goes wild, but I don't pay them any attention as I kiss Catalina. I pour my everything into our kiss—every single ounce of yearning I've felt toward her, along with all the hopes I have about the following year.

A year I want to spend with her, so long as she wants the same.

The kiss morphs from sweet to desperate to lazy before we're both forcing ourselves to pull away. I'm not sure I would've if it weren't for Aiden clapping me on the back before dragging us out of the bar and onto Main Street, where he spent a pretty penny hiring some college kids to put on a fireworks show for Gaby.

Catalina and I both sip champagne while watching the sky light up with a thousand sparkling lights. Or more like she watches while I spend most of the show watching her.

I swear to myself in that moment that I'll do everything in my power to keep that look of pure wonder on her face. That I'll fight my hardest to show her that what we have can form into something great, even if it means overcoming every obstacle in our way.

There isn't a single doubt in my mind that I could fall in love with this girl. In fact, I hope I do.

Just like I hope she can love me back.

CHAPTER TWENTY-SIX

Catalina

My two suitcases drag behind me like a lead block as I make my way through the Los Angeles airport. Despite being excited to see Monica, there is a heaviness in my limbs that I'm unaccustomed to, and a dull throb is building behind my temples when I think about starting my new job tomorrow. The position might be temporary, but the growing ache in my chest feels like it is only beginning.

I do my best to push my oppressive thoughts aside once I step outside. Monica's blond hair and bright athletic set makes her easy to spot, and I rush over to her. She pulls me into her arms, and thankfully, some of the tension in my body bleeds away.

"I'm so excited that you're here!" She opens her trunk and helps me place my luggage inside.

"Me too." I try my best to sound excited, but the statement seems to be lacking based on the way she

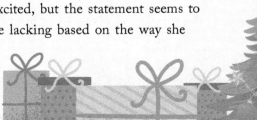

looks at me.

"Missing Luke already?"

"No," I say unconvincingly.

Yes, I miss him, but admitting it aloud to Monica is nearly as hard as coming to terms with it myself. It seems silly to miss someone I have only just started to get to know, but then again, he made sure I saw him almost every day over the last two weeks. His efforts to make me crave his company appear to have worked a little too well, and now I'm left wondering how the hell I'm going to make it through three months away from him.

Assuming you find a job near Lake Wisteria in twelve weeks.

My stomach clenches as worry worms its way into my heart.

"I think I know just the thing to cheer you up." Monica's chipper voice draws me out of my head.

"What?"

"Burgers and the beach!"

"How's the apartment?" Luke asks.

"Good." I readjust the volume on my earbuds so I can hear him better while I mill about, organizing my sparse number of items, each in its rightful place.

"Is it as nice as you remember?"

I look around the sublease. There is a peekaboo view of the ocean, which makes up for the older furnishings and outdated kitchen and bathroom. I was shocked to see that the same studio apartment I rented a year prior was available again, and while it hasn't changed much since my last stay, I can't say the same about myself.

"It's a little more run-down."

"At least the view is good?"

I stare out the window. "Yeah."

"I'm looking forward to seeing it."

His comment perks me up a bit. "When do you think you'll visit?"

He chuckles to himself. "I need to coordinate with the hospital and Aiden, but I'm hoping by the end of the month."

My happiness fades. "Oh."

"Disappointed it's not sooner?"

Yes, but I'm not about to admit that aloud. "I'm going to be so busy these next few weeks, so it's probably for the best."

Right. You keep telling yourself that and maybe you'll finally start believing it.

"Time will fly by. Just you wait and see."

Time doesn't fly by. Instead, I feel like I'm trapped inside an hourglass, counting each individual grain of sand as the days go by excruciatingly slowly.

I've missed home before. It's hard not to after growing up in a town like Lake Wisteria, surrounded by people who have known me since before I was born. Sure, I've enjoyed traveling, but the more I think about it, the less I want to stay away from my hometown.

Up until now, I was happy about moving around and filling in for nurses around the United States. I've been able to explore new places, put myself out there, and meet a ton of new people, all of which were difficult tasks for me before becoming a travel nurse.

I've grown up in so many ways, but perhaps it's time for another change. One that begins with returning to the place where my whole life began and to the man who lives there.

Doctor Darling.

I rub my eyes to double-check that I'm not seeing things.

"Luke?"

He doesn't give me a chance to process the fact that he is here in California before his mouth crushes against mine. His kiss is a claiming one that leaves an invisible mark long after he pulls away, and one I can't stop replaying as I let him inside my apartment.

"I know you don't like surprises, but I hope you don't mind this one." He drags his luggage inside before I throw myself into his arms.

"Are you kidding?" I ask between kisses. "This is the best one ever."

His smirk makes my stomach muscles clench. "So, you don't mind?"

"I only mind that you're doubting me."

He drops a kiss on my mouth in a silent apology. "I wasn't sure—"

I shut him up by my mouth pressing against his. "Less talking. More reuniting."

"No need to tell me twice." His fingers comb through my

hair before his hands cradle the back of my head, holding me in place while he shows me just how much he missed me.

We spend a couple of hours in bed together before we make our way back into the living room to eat pizza from a local spot I like before cuddling on the couch and putting on a movie.

I curl into Luke's side with a sigh. "How long are you staying?"

He frowns. "I'm flying back tomorrow night."

My elation fades away. "Oh."

"But I can come back soon."

"And I can visit at least once."

The line between his brows smooths out. "Do you have any plans for where you're going next?"

I try to stifle my smile and fail. "I have a few options."

His rare scowl returns with a vengeance. "That's…good."

"Is it?"

His arms tighten around my waist. "Of course. You love your job."

I trace my finger down his chest, earning a soft little inhale from him. "I do."

"And it pays well."

"Can't complain about that."

"Right." A vein in his neck strains.

"But…"

His gaze locks onto mine. "But?"

"There is one big con."

"I'm listening."

"It's only been a few weeks, and I'm already thinking about the next time I get to go back to Lake Wisteria."

"That can be arranged."

I straddle his lap and cup his cheeks. "Really?"

"I've been keeping an eye on any job listings at the hospital."

My smile is instantaneous. "Have you?"

His hands on my hips secure me in place. "Nothing yet, but I'm hopeful. Apparently, one of the NICU nurses is going on maternity leave in three months."

My heart threatens to burst at the idea of Luke stalking job opportunities for me. "Miss me that much?"

"A concerning amount to say the least."

"Is there such a thing?"

"Yes, but only because I have no idea when I'll get to see you again."

I lean forward and capture his mouth. "I can say for certain I'll be moving back to Lake Wisteria after I'm done with this job."

He wrenches himself away. "What?"

"I decided before you showed up."

"And you waited until now to tell me?"

I laugh. "You didn't give me much of a chance."

One moment, I'm straddling Luke's lap, and the next, I'm being tossed over his shoulder as he takes me back to the bedroom.

"We're back to this?"

He smacks my ass, and I hiss between my gritted teeth.

"What was that for?"

"Waiting until now to tell me that you're coming home."

Home has never sounded better than it does in this moment, and my heart throbs in a silent reply.

"I take it you're happy?"

He throws me on the bed before joining me. "I spent the whole plane ride coming up with this elaborate plan to convince you to come back, and for what?"

I can't help grinning. "Do tell me more."

His eyes narrow. "You're being a little too smug about all this."

"Can you blame a girl for wanting to hear all about how much you miss her?"

"Depends on if she admits to missing me too."

I circle my arms around the back of his neck and tug him closer. "I missed you as soon as I got here."

"You never said anything."

"And risk you thinking I was too clingy?"

"There's no such thing."

I roll my eyes. "Sure."

He tucks his hand under my chin and forces me to look at him. "I like knowing you're obsessed with me."

I shove his shoulder with a laugh. "I'm not obsessed."

"That's not how I interpreted it."

"It's not my fault you lack the ability to analyze context clues."

"Except all my clues lead to one theory."

"What?"

"That you're falling in love with me."

My cheeks flame. "Shut up."

"It's okay if you are. It'll be our little secret."

"That's great, but I'm not."

His smile stretches further. "Then why is your face turning red?"

"Because you're embarrassing me!"

"What's to be embarrassed about? I'm an extremely lovable person."

"Keep talking and I'll question if that's the case."

He rolls us over so I'm straddled on top of him. "For the record, I think it's cute when you get all shy."

"While we're taking notes, I'll have you know that I hated every second of this conversation."

"Should we table it for a later time?"

"Yes," I say with a hiss.

He nods. "Fine. I'll be crossing off *dramatic love confession* from the dream board."

I lean forward until our faces are only a few inches apart. "Luke?"

"Yes?"

"Stop talking and kiss me already before I change my mind about moving back."

His mischievous smile makes my stomach dip. "Your wish is my command."

shake it before
you taste it

EPILOGUE
Catalina

Two Years Later

After a rough night at the Lake Aurora hospital, I spend the short drive back to Luke's and my apartment dreaming of my boyfriend's arms wrapped around me—only to be met with silence when I unlock the front door and step inside our small but welcoming home. Luke left a side table lamp on for me, but the couch where he usually falls asleep while waiting for me is empty.

"Luke?" I search the kitchen, bedroom, and bathroom for him, but my call remains unanswered, further adding to my disappointment.

Spending the last year living with Luke has clearly spoiled me. Somewhere between falling in love and moving in together, I forgot what it felt like to be alone. Now that I remember the unsettling feeling that plagued me for years,

I'm even more grateful for Luke's love, companionship, and ability to make the worst days a little more bearable.

Before hopping in the shower, I text Luke to ask where he is, but he doesn't reply to my message. I distract myself by heating up some leftovers he saved me, scrolling through and commenting on the photos my sister sent me of nursery ideas she is considering, and letting my brain rot for a few minutes on social media.

I'm so distracted by a video of a dog being reunited with its long-lost owner that I don't hear Luke unlocking the front door until it is already slamming shut behind him.

I pop my head out of the kitchen. "What were you up—" My question dies as my gaze drops to the massive rectangular box in his arms. "Oh my God."

His beaming smile expands even wider. "Surprise?"

I run up to him and throw my arms around his neck, ignoring the LEGO set pressing against his chest. "How did you get one?"

He kisses the top of my head. "I waited in line for over ten hours and hoped I would get lucky."

I blink twice. "You waited ten hours?"

"Yes."

"By yourself?" I grab his hand and drag him over to the couch.

"Aiden kept me company for part of it."

"Why did he ditch you?"

"Why else?" He arches a brow.

I grab the box from Luke's hands and place it on the table before straddling his lap. He grips my hips, holding me in place while I pepper his cheeks with soft kisses.

"I take it you're happy?"

"Are you seriously asking me that? I never thought we stood a chance at getting one." I tip my head in the direction of the new limited-edition LEGO set of our favorite science fiction cinematic universe. Ever since we finished the Galactic Command Base, we've been slowly collecting and building the sets from the same fictional world, although I never imagined Luke would manage to get us this one.

According to the frequently asked questions page on their website, there were only a few hundred thousand made in the whole world, which sounds like a lot until people consider the popularity of the movies.

"I had to try." His beaming smile is infectious, and I find myself returning his with one of my own. It's astonishing how only a few minutes in Luke's presence eases the oppressive sadness that has been following me ever since I found out my patient wasn't responding well to their treatment.

"What's wrong?" He cups my cheek.

"I didn't say anything."

"You don't have to." He readjusts our positions until I'm settled against his side, tucked protectively under his arm.

I sink into him with a sigh.

"Rough day?" He asks.

"Yeah."

"Want to talk about it?"

"Not exactly."

His arm tightens around me. "I'm sorry."

"For what?"

"I wish I could take away whatever has you looking so…" He scans my face with a small frown.

I don't bother concealing my true feelings with a reassuring smile meant to put him at ease. The truth is that death is a dark part of the medical profession. Denying the reality doesn't make it any easier, but knowing I have Luke to come home to…

I couldn't ask for a better friend, lover, and life partner.

"Thank you," I blurt out without any context.

His brows pinch together. "What for?"

I clasp his chin. "Being you."

"You give me too much credit for doing the bare minimum."

I point at the LEGO box. "Are we pretending that you didn't stand in line for ten hours to get that?"

"I'd do it all over again to see the smile on your face when you saw it."

My heart thumps harder in my chest. I disguise the way his words turn my insides to mush with an eye roll. "Will you ever stop being so sappy?"

"Depends on how long you plan on loving me."

"Now that you mention it…"

He brushes the ticklish spot between my ribs that always makes me laugh and kick my feet.

"Stop!"

"I take personal offense to that statement."

"Well, you did emphasize the importance of being honest—"

He twists our bodies until I'm trapped beneath him with my spine pressing into the couch cushion and him hovering above me.

"Emphasis on the honesty," he says with a little hiss.

"I think I could love you forever."

"You. Think?" He annunciates each word.

I swallow my laugh. "I'm still not entirely convinced."

"Is there anything I can do to sway you either way?"

"Perhaps."

"I have a few ideas." He grabs my left hand and brushes his mouth over my ringless finger. A small shudder courses through me, a fact that doesn't go unnoticed by the man I love, given the way his eyes spark with interest.

"And here I thought you wanted to wait another year."

"What?" I sputter. "When did I say that?"

His brow arches. "So, you *do* want to get married?"

"Obviously."

"To me?"

"After this conversation, I'm questioning it."

His bright smile sends a wave of warmth through me. "But you *have* thought about it."

I push at his chest with a frustrated grunt. "Stop teasing me."

He drops a quick kiss on my mouth. "Never."

"You're annoying."

"And you're being oddly evasive over a single question."

"Because I'm not about to admit the truth."

"That you're madly in love with me and have been painting your nails white for the last couple of months, hoping that I'll pop the question."

My death glare doesn't deter him from continuing.

He brushes my flushed cheek with the pad of his thumb. "For what it's worth, I think it's cute."

My eyes screw shut. "Please have the decency to let me die of embarrassment in peace."

"The likelihood of that happening is slim to none."

"Unfortunately," I say with a sigh.

"I was waiting for the right moment," he says after a few seconds of silence.

"The right moment?" I stare up at him, confused.

"I kept talking myself out of it and coming up with reasons why it wasn't the best time."

Oh. My. God.

His cheeks flush. "Aiden told me I was being stupid, and looking back on it, he was right."

My heart, which was furiously pounding only a few moments ago, stops. "What?"

"One second." Luke disappears into our bedroom before returning with a...

I sit up and squint. "What is that?"

"Something I made." He kneels in front of me and holds out the dark box made out of small LEGOs.

"Is that..." I can't even finish my sentence.

"A ring box?"

I cover my gaping mouth with the palm of my hand and nod.

"Yes."

"You made that?"

Luke nods, and tears spring to my eyes. I'm not entirely sure what he says after that, in part because my heart is beating so loudly that I can hardly hear his speech over the whooshing sound of blood pumping in my ears, but I swear the look on his face says it all.

"Will you marry me?"

I look down at the ring nestled inside the box he built just for me. Choosing to love him for the rest of my life is the easiest decision I've ever made—almost as easy as saying one little word.

"Yes."

THE END

AUTHOR'S NOTE

If you made it to this note, I just want to say thank you for taking a chance on "My December Darling". It's my first completely indie published release in a long time, so I appreciate your support.

Honestly, I never imagined writing a novella because have you seen the size of my books' spines? My usual word count goal is 100,000 words, so keeping this one under 50,000 was an exciting challenge. Although the holiday novella was close to becoming a full-length book (not sure who made all these rules), I was somehow able to keep it short and sweet (and prove to my closest friends and myself that I could do it!).

*Note: I had originally planned to not have a spicy scene in the book because I wanted my family to be able to read it too, but I felt like I really wanted to write this one, so here we are.

"My December Darling" was a pleasant surprise. No one expected this kind of story from me, which meant I was able to have fun and write without any of the usual pressure I put on myself. Don't get me wrong. I always have enjoy working on my projects, and this one was no different, but I needed a story like this after writing "Love Unwritten".

Departing from my typical billionaire trope was equally fun. One of the main reasons I wanted to tell this kind of story was because I write about so many billionaires. While Luke Darling might not have 50 million to spend during a charity auction like Declan Kane or own half of Lake Wisteria like the Lopez cousins, he will stand in line for hours to buy you a limited-edition LEGO set, so he's worth a billion dollars in my heart.

I feel like there are so many more stories I could tell in the world of Lake Wisteria, so I don't imagine this is the end. The small, lakefront town has become one of my favorite fictional places, and I hope you feel the same way.

If you're interested in reading more small-town romances from me, you can check out my Lakefront Billionaires series.

Going to go shamelessly listen to holiday music now,

Lauren

ALSO BY LAUREN ASHER...

LAKEFRONT BILLIONAIRES SERIES
A series of interconnected standalones
Love Redesigned
Love Unwritten
Love Arranged

DREAMLAND BILLIONAIRES SERIES
A series of interconnected standalones
The Fine Print
Terms and Conditions
Final Offer

DIRTY AIR SERIES
A series of interconnected standalones
Throttled
Collided
Wrecked
Redeemed

Scan the code to read the books

ACKNOWLEDGEMENTS

Kimberly Brower—I'm not sure this book would've existed without you, so thank you for encouraging me to explore new opportunities and challenge myself as an author. I'm so grateful that you were put in my life because I can't imagine this author journey without you!

Aimee and the team at Brower Literary—I'm so appreciative of the hard work you put into making each of my books a success.

To Nina, Kim, and the team at VPR—Thanks for all you do to keep my head on straight with each release.

Mary a.k.a. my Finneas—Thank you for bringing so much joy to my life and being my yellow person. I'm so honored to not only call you the GOAT when it comes to graphic design, but also one of my dearest friends.

Jos, the future Mrs. Darling—Thank you never feels like enough for all you do and all the happiness you bring me each day! I can always count on you to be in my corner, keeping me calm and reminding me of all the good things that come with each project we work on together. Your peptalk voicenotes during this one have become a core memory for me and encouraged me to hit publish (along with the crying selfies).

Erica—From my very first self-published book to this one, each one is sentimental in its own way because I get to work with you and share the joy of something new together. Your passion, empathy, and endless championing for your authors makes you such a joy to work with, and I'm happy we will have many more projects together.

To my mitten state representative, Katelyn—Thank you for teaching me all about Midwest living and why driving McLarens in the wintertime is a bad idea. When I visited Michigan this year (and met you and your family), I truly felt the midwest magic, and you're a part of the reason why.

Marietere—I've been thinking about writing this type of holiday book for a while, so I'm incredibly happy that we could collaborate on this one together and that you could help me represent my Puerto Rican readers in the best way.

Kendra—With each project we work on together, I become even more grateful to have met you. Your care and kindness have truly made such an impact on me while navigating this book space, and I'm already hoping I can see you again soon to give you a hug!

Selina—Thank you for helping me with all the medical elements! Your feedback really put me at ease, and I'm so very appreciative of all your support!

To my beta readers—You're such an essential part of my process, and without you, I most likely wouldn't have the confidence to put these books out into the world, so thank you for believing in me and helping me make each book that much more special.

To my mother-in-law—I love your stories about the parrandas so much that I was inspired to write about them. It took me a few years, but I'm glad I could finally share some love for the AGDO family.

Printed in the USA
CPSIA information can be obtained
at www.ICGtesting.com
LVHW022244171124
796794LV00009BA/35